SHERLOCK HOLMES: THE FOUR-HANDED GAME

Holmes and Watson find themselves bombarded with an avalanche of dramatic cases! Holmes enrols Inspectors Lestrade and Bradstreet to help him play a dangerous four-handed game against an organization whose power and influence seems to know no bounds. As dissimilar as the cases seem to be — robbery, assault, and gruesome murder — Holmes suspects that each one has been meticulously designed to lure him towards a conclusion that even he could not have anticipated. However, when his brother Mycroft goes missing, he realizes that he is running out of time . . .

PAUL D. GILBERT

SHERLOCK HOLMES: THE FOUR-HANDED GAME

Complete and Unabridged

LINFORD
Leicester

First published in Great Britain in 2017 by
Robert Hale
an imprint of The Crowood Press
Wiltshire

First Linford Edition
published 2019
by arrangement with
The Crowood Press
Wiltshire

A catalogue record for this book is available
from the British Library.

ISBN 978–1–4448–4144–2

Published by
F. A. Thorpe (Publishing)
Anstey, Leicestershire

Set by Words & Graphics Ltd.
Anstey, Leicestershire
Printed and bound in Great Britain by
T. J. International Ltd., Padstow, Cornwall

This book is printed on acid-free paper

Contents

Introduction

The response that I have received to *The Unholy Trinity* has led me to fly headlong into my latest book with an unprecedented enthusiasm. Consequently I will not prevail upon your patience for any longer than it takes to express my sincerest gratitude to both my publishers and my readers for making my latest effort at all possible.

I can report that the enthusiasm of my wife, Jackie, remains undiminished and as always, her advice and support have proved to be invaluable.

PDG

Foreword

My friend, Sherlock Holmes, has long maintained that his constitution is well able to withstand any amount and degree of vigour in the pursuit of his art, so long as he is continually fed with work and stimulation.

I can assure you that this maxim of his was more than ably put to the test during the course of the weeks that immediately followed our return from Egypt and Italy. In a rapid succession that bordered on the uncanny, problems that were too intriguing for even he to turn away were presented to our door at 221b Baker Street.

Any professional objections that I might have raised as to the threat to his health that such a workload presented inevitably proved to be futile and of course, fell upon deaf ears. The effect of our adventures abroad and their dramatic conclusions upon our return to London would have been enough to have exhausted and dissipated any ordinary man. However, the energy and enthusiasm that Holmes threw into each one of these extraordinary cases appeared to be almost superhuman!

I threw up my arms in despair and as you would expect, offered my limited assistance and support, in any fashion that I was able. As Holmes' biographer, or as he often referred to me, his Boswell, I was indeed fortunate that each one of these cases afforded him the opportunity to display his considerable gifts and powers to their fullest extent.

Little did I realize that the resolution of these cases would have consequences that I would not have otherwise conceived of . . .

J. H. Watson

Prologue:

The Guardian of the Scrolls

For those among you who have yet to read my account of the Unholy Trinity[1] affair, I thought it best that I provide an outline of the events that have preceded the adventure of the Four-Handed Game.

Holmes and I had been enjoying a most leisurely breakfast when our door was sent crashing from its hinges, revealing a gigantic and colourfully dressed Bedouin wielding a colossal sword. The Bedouin issued us with a violent warning; that if we were to interfere with the affairs of his people we would run the risk of facing fatal consequences. To emphasize his point, the Bedouin sliced my dining chair clean in two, with a single blow!

To my surprise, for once Holmes seemed to be as ignorant of the reason for this warning as I had been and all we

1

could do was speculate as to the Bedouin's motives. Meanwhile Holmes despatched two of his mysterious wires. Holmes' observations and deductions only revealed that the Bedouin had arrived from the Continent recently, but more significantly he had also noticed that this giant had been sporting a symbol of the ancient Coptic Church.

At this point Holmes received a written request from Cardinal Pietro, a confidant of his Holiness the Pope, requesting that we should journey to the Vatican with all speed to investigate the mysterious death of Pietro's colleague, Cardinal Tosca.[2] After a long but largely uneventful journey, we were finally met at the station in Rome by our old friend, Inspector Gialli, who had worked by our sides during the Dying Gaul[3] affair.

An examination of Tosca's office revealed that he had been scrutinizing a controversial and ancient Coptic scroll, a portion of which had been removed at the time of his murder. Tosca's throat had been slit by the curved blade of an enormous sword and everything indicated that the culprit had been none other than the enormous Bedouin who had ransacked 221b Baker Street!

Holmes was convinced that the solution to this crime lay within the parchment of the missing scrolls and Inspector Gialli immediately agreed to obtain a translation to aid Holmes in his investigation. On his way to the translator, Gialli had been set upon by two Englishmen dressed in identical brown suits and they beat him to within an inch of his life, before making off with the scrolls. Gialli had been rendered incapable of giving any sort of evidence for a considerable time, so Holmes decided that the best way of continuing his quest for the truth would be to visit an ancient Coptic church in Egypt.

Holmes asked me to return to London with all speed for he now feared for the safety of Mrs Hudson, while he intended to travel on to Egypt without me. Obviously I tried to dissuade Holmes from undertaking such a venture on his own, but Holmes assured me that he would be liaising with his old friend,

Elradji of the Egyptian police.

Nevertheless, I decided to attempt the unthinkable. I actually believed that I could deceive Holmes by wiring his brother Mycroft and asking him to keep a close on eye on Mrs Hudson while I followed Holmes to Egypt in a makeshift disguise! Mycroft reluctantly agreed to cooperate with my scheme, even though he was unconvinced of my potential success. However, I was also aware of the fact that he appeared to be showing an unusual interest in the whole affair.

Throughout that long and arduous journey to 'the cradle of civilization', I was constantly on my guard because Holmes was being kept under very close surveillance by two Bedouins, in similar attire to that sported by our uninvited London visitor. Their attention did not appear to be born of a friendly disposition, so I made sure that Holmes was never out of my sight for more than a moment or two.

We travelled by train to Brindisi, then by ferry to Alexandria and finally by train once more, on to Cairo. It was in the midst of a vast and crowded bazaar that I observed Holmes conferring with his friend Elradji. Seemingly intent on acting upon Elradji's advice, Holmes immediately boarded a *felucca*[4] that was sailing upstream along the fabled River Nile. I obtained a similar craft of my own and soon we were in hot but discreet pursuit.

The skipper of my felucca, Taharka, had overheard Holmes request a speedy passage to the famous Hanging Church of St Mary, which had been built upon the site of the most ancient Coptic church[5] in the world.

However, when I went ashore I found that Holmes was nowhere to be seen. I searched high and low for him, but after I had taken directions to the fabled church I thought that my search for Holmes was a lost cause. However, to my great embarrassment, he soon revealed himself to me in a disguise of his own and told me that he had first noticed me when we had boarded the train from Rome to Brindisi!

As we were about to enter the church, I noticed a cloud of sand bearing down towards us and I only had seconds in which to hurl Holmes out of the way of two marauding horsemen! His gratitude at my having saved his life dispelled some of my earlier embarrassment.

We were greeted at the entrance to the church by an elderly monk called Shenouda, who made us most welcome. We spent two days and nights in his company, during which time he explained why the contents of the scrolls might appear controversial.

The scrolls contained extracts of the lost Gospel of Mary Magdalene,[6] which painted an entirely different aspect of the scriptures from the version that was generally accepted. He told us that the discovery of this scroll could be most damaging to the Catholic Church, which is why Cardinal Tosca purchased them from the well-known thief, Hashmoukh of Akhmim, a small, ancient town located further down the river.

Shenouda expressed his surprise that Tosca was found studying the scrolls, rather than having them destroyed as one would have expected. He must have paid an enormous price in acquiring them, for Hashmoukh normally sold his ill-gotten wares to a private collector and theologian in London — Professor Ronald Sydney.[7]

Shenouda was shocked to see our reaction to this news, because he was not aware of the attack upon Inspector Gialli by two gentlemen also from London. However, Holmes and I were slowly becoming aware of the enormous sweep and influence that Professor Sydney truly had. His quest for Mary's Gospel knew no bounds and with that in mind Holmes decided to find out more from the thief, Hashmoukh.

Before taking our leave of Shenouda he summoned his servant Akhom, who would act as both our guide and bodyguard throughout the remainder of our time in Egypt. We were both dumbstruck when, in answer to Shenouda's summons, a gigantic Bedouin entered the room. Akhom was none other than our violent visitor in London! As it transpired, his had been a friendly warning, because Shenouda had been well aware of the danger that we were likely to face during our quest.

Akhom was as good as his word, and he followed our every step from Cairo to Akhmim, where we were met at the jetty by Elradji. He guided us to the ramshackle home of Hashmoukh, only to find that the thief's throat had also been severed from ear to ear.

Our journey to Akhmim had not been entirely in vain however, because Holmes had discovered a calling card lying on a soiled side table, which bore the name of Professor Sydney. After saying our farewells to Elradji and Taharka, the impressive Nubian felucca pilot who had been so invaluable to us, we finally took our leave of Egypt.

Akhom duly fulfilled his duties at the station of Alexandria, saving Holmes and I from near certain death at the hands of those ever present Bedouins who had been marking our every step. He despatched them both with his sword, but Holmes and Elradji ensured that he escaped prosecution for those violent deaths on the grounds of self-defence.

As a postscript to our time in Egypt, we discovered shortly after our return to London that even the aged Shenouda could not escape the long arm of Professor Sydney and the unholy trinity. Sadly, he had met with the same ghastly fate as had Hashmoukh and the news of his death affected Holmes badly.

Upon our return to Rome, Holmes provided some vital clues to the slowly recovering Gialli, which would ensure the implication of Cardinal Pietro in the death of Cardinal Tosca. Although Pietro's position within the Vatican would not permit his prosecution, within a few days he was despatched to an isolated mission in central Africa from which he would never be able to return. Cardinal Pietro and Sydney were undoubtedly two members of the trinity, but who was the third?

Holmes deduced that the culmination of our search would be realized in London and we initiated our departure from Rome without delay. It was on the penultimate stretch of our journey home, namely the train from Turin to Paris, that we became aware of the presence on board of the two men in brown suits who had so brutally attacked Inspector Gialli. Holmes and I foiled their deadly attack upon us and they remained secure until the police removed them from the train in Paris to be returned to Rome for prosecution.

Upon our return to London, Holmes and I were immediately thrown into an unusual case of murder at the request of our old friend, Inspector Lestrade. At first it seemed as if our enquiries were going to act as a welcome diversion from our all-consuming quest. However, as we delved deeper into the intrigue surrounding Lestrade's case, we began to realize that both cases were somehow connected.

Piece by piece, Holmes and I forged a connection between the murder of Christophe Decaux; Mycroft's club the Diogenes and the Bavarian Brotherhood. Decaux, his murderer Roger Ashley, Dr Marcus Harding (who we discovered had falsified Decaux's post mortem report) and Sir Oswald Austin-Simons, the lawyer entrusted with the case of Ashley, were all members of the Diogenes Club and close friends and associates of Professor Ronald Sydney!

Furthermore, we subsequently discovered that Austin-Simons had somehow engineered the release of the men in brown suits who had been extradited back to London. At this juncture Holmes decided to take Lestrade fully into our confidence and the man from Scotland Yard had been so impressed and shocked by these revelations, that he decided to throw in his lot with us and turned a blind eye to some of Holmes' more unconventional methods.

All this while, Holmes had been impatiently awaiting the arrival of vital replies to three wires that he had despatched. Two were from colleagues of his in Bavaria and the other from his brother Mycroft. Holmes refused to comment upon the two from Bavaria, but the absence of a reply from his brother prompted him to seek one in person.

In Holmes' absence I began to speculate on how involved in these intrigues Mycroft actually was. After all, the reply that I had received from him in Egypt was enigmatic to say the least and he had even been aware of the exact time of our arrival back in London. My reverie was soon interrupted by the arrival of Inspector Lestrade, who had received a message from Holmes. We two were to await directions and instruction from our colleague and cab driver, Dave 'Gunner' King, who was to bring us to Holmes at the specified time.

Our wait extended well into the early hours of the following day, when King finally arrived to drive us to a rendezvous at the museum in Bloomsbury, where Sydney ran the department of ancient manuscripts.

Our liaison with Holmes in the museum's courtyard culminated in an ambush attempt upon Professor Sydney and his two henchmen, the irrepressible men in brown suits. However, Sydney's knowledge of the geography of the museum almost thwarted our scheme and only the timely intervention of Gunner King managed to save the day. A long and nerve-shredding gun battle ensued between the seven of us and it was some time before the smoke lifted to reveal the shocking aftermath.

Sydney's henchmen had both fallen; one under the wheels and hooves of King's cab and the other from a bullet from my revolver. Lestrade had suffered a minor flesh wound while Holmes and I remained unscathed. A bullet from Holmes had brought Sydney to the point of death, but with his final, blood-soaked breath he was able to issue Holmes with a sinister threat. Despite his death, the order that he served would not be denied!

We returned to Baker Street in a state of exhaustion, but once Holmes had retired to his room, I discovered two sheets of paper within the fire grate that Holmes had unwittingly left untouched by the flames. Holmes had summarized the contents of the wires to me earlier, but it was the crest on one of them that had intrigued me the most. An unusual depiction of an owl formed part of this crest and it seemed to be strangely familiar to me.

The owl had been featured in the hand

of Athena, as part of an oil landscape that I had once noticed upon the wall of Mycroft Holmes' office . . .

1

The Regular Passenger

During the course of the weeks that had immediately followed our dramatic return from Egypt and Rome, I had noted with some amusement the voracious manner in which my friend, Sherlock Holmes, had attacked each example of Mrs Hudson's limited cuisine.

This fact is only worthy of note because Holmes' mealtime habits were normally far more ascetic than they had been of late. This was especially true when he was engaged on a difficult case and he could therefore ill afford to expend the energy that was required for his mental faculties on a matter as trifling as the digestion of food!

One morning, during the course of a particularly cold and windy period that had been plaguing the October of 1896, Holmes looked up from his plate and observed my amusement through a suspicious eye. He had just devoured a substantial plate of devilled kidneys and eggs and he was in the process of wiping up the residue with a slice of bread, when his observation caused him to toss his fork down onto his plate with some annoyance.

'Really Watson, I am surprised that after all of these years in my association you have not yet learned the simple truth, that there is nothing more harmful to a logical thinking process than to make false assumptions before one is in possession of the facts!'

I was on the point of questioning the cause of his fractious outburst, when I realized the futility of such an enquiry. Holmes obviously had every intention of expanding upon his initial assertion, for he promptly stood up, strode over to the window and struck a match for his cigarette with unwarranted violence. The flame almost flared onto the drapes and his next few words were clouded in a plume of smoke.

He moved away from the window and

turned upon me while pointing with his cigarette.

'On more occasions than I care to remember, you have berated me for my abstinence during a long and arduous case, little realizing how beneficial this can be to my faculties. Now you have formulated the notion that, because I am not gainfully employed at the moment, I am merely eating to compensate for my lack of activity.' Holmes shook his head dismissively while putting his cigarette to his lips once more.

'It has not even occurred to you that our adventure abroad might have drained even I of every drop of the mental and physical energies that I possess. Perhaps I am eating so ravenously of late merely because I am hungry. To assume that my dining habits have changed because I am being starved of work is to dismiss the thought that I might actually be glad of this temporary respite. However, as you will soon see, it is also a grave error! Hah!' With a broad smile Holmes suddenly held up a small sheet of paper tantalizingly in front of me.

'Now deduce, friend Watson, do not assume!'

'You have a client,' I stated flatly.

'Indeed I do, a John Vincent Harden[1] to be precise and he is due to arrive to seek our consultation in precisely five minutes time! Mrs Hudson!' Holmes called for our landlady to clear away our breakfast things with an understandable urgency and he soon hustled her from the room again once she had carried out her task.

'Our consultation?' I queried, for I had often remonstrated with Holmes at the way he took for granted my participation, without prior invitation.

'Well, if you would be so kind, allowing, of course, for any previous commitment that might inhibit you.' Holmes smiled, fully aware of my current status and therefore of the nature of my final response.

'I would be honoured,' I confirmed with a smile, 'and I will fetch my notebook at once!'

I returned in an instant and there was even a moment or two for me to look over Harden's short note of introduction prior to his arrival. There was little of significance within Harden's brief request, save for a hint of urgency in its tone. Inevitably, Holmes' appraisal was at total variance to my own.

'These few words certainly tell us much about the man who wrote them, would you not say, Doctor?'

I was no doubt exhibiting an expression of confusion, for Holmes continued without awaiting my nonplussed response.

'Look at the care that has gone into the formation of each of his letters. Each twist and curve is accurate and precise and there is not a dot or a cross that misses its mark. It is reassuring at the commencement of any case, Watson, to realize that we are dealing with a person of a remarkable nature. You can be assured of the accuracy of John Vincent Harden's evidence!' Holmes pronounced.

'Not to mention his punctuality,' I confirmed, for at the very moment of his appointed time we could hear Mrs Hudson greeting our new client at the door to 221b Baker Street. At that moment I recalled where I had heard his name before and I hurriedly reminded Holmes that Harden was one of the most powerful men in the tobacco industry.

Barely a second later John Vincent Harden walked tentatively into our room and Holmes leapt up to greet him with a broad and charming smile. At once Holmes could sense the elderly gentleman's apprehension and hesitancy.

'Calm yourself Mr Harden!' Holmes declared. 'Have no fear, for I can assure you that you are amongst friends. Perhaps a cup of coffee will have the desired reassuring effect?'

I decided to save Mrs Hudson from being subjected to one of Holmes' strident orders and I called down quietly from the top of the landing for a tray of coffee.

By the time that I had returned to the room, Harden was already perched somewhat uneasily on the edge of our visitor's chair while Holmes was busy filling his cherry wood pipe. No one uttered a single word until after the coffee had been safely delivered and Holmes had ushered our landlady from the room, in his usual unceremonious fashion.

Once his pipe was fully alight, Holmes turned towards our guest and with an ironic grin he held the note of introduction immediately in front of our client's face.

'Mr Harden, your letter was somewhat scant of detail,' Holmes stated in an accusing tone.

'I apologize for that, Mr Holmes, but I was certain that if I had betrayed even one word of the nature of this affair, prior to my arrival, you would have surely and immediately dismissed me as some kind of madman and consequently refused to grant me this interview.'

Harden's explanation immediately fuelled Holmes' love of the unusual and bizarre and his attitude visibly softened as a brief smile of satisfaction played upon his lips.

I took my notebook over to my chair and immediately observed how perfectly Harden's appearance mirrored the pedantic nature of his note. Despite his advanced years, for he was surely not a day younger than sixty-five, Harden was impeccably turned out. His worsted suit had clearly been hand tailored, his tie and shoes were equally immaculate and his neatly clipped moustache and grey thinning hair told of a very recent visit to the barber's shop. When he spoke each word was clipped and precise.

Holmes took to his chair, while his keen eyes did not leave our client's face for an instant.

'Now Mr Harden, I implore you to recount, as exactly as you can, the events and circumstances that have led you to seek my advice upon this matter. You may also be assured that you can rely as much upon Dr Watson's discretion, as you can upon my own.

'Please bear in mind that, apart from the very obvious facts that you smoke a very expensive brand of Havana cigar without a holder, that you have recently retired from the tobacco industry and that you travel extensively upon the Metropolitan railway, I know nothing about you whatsoever!'

Upon completing this astonishing statement, Holmes turned his face away from our client, ostensibly to light his pipe but also no doubt so that he might evade the inevitable looks of admiration and amazement upon our faces, that he often found to be so tiresome.

His precaution was certainly warranted, for the reaction of both Harden and myself was precisely the one that Holmes had sought to avoid. Harden also added voice to his astonishment.

'Mr Holmes!' he exclaimed. 'Thanks to Dr Watson here, I have read so many accounts of your remarkable talents that I did not expect to be so dumfounded by anything that I might have heard here today. I beseech you to explain yourself sir, for it is almost as if you knew of me already.'

Holmes was barely able to subdue a smile of self-satisfaction upon hearing Harden's words of veneration, although he was also clearly irritated by this slight delay to the proceedings. Consequently his response was as curt as it was brief. He turned abruptly towards our client and demonstrated his explanation by pointing towards the tips of Harden's fingers.

'The browning of your fingertips betrays the fact that you despise the prevailing trend for the use of cigar holders while the light dusting of ash on your shoulder indicates the brand. As Watson will assure you, I have made an extensive study of cigar and cigarette ash and its use in the detection of crime and the residues of Havanas are very distinctive. Your hat bears a thin layer of a type of soot that is unique to the Metropolitan railway and your gold watch and chain indicate your very recent retirement.'

In answer to our questioning glances, Holmes then added, 'The initials on the back of your watch, HTI, surely stand for Harden Tobacco Industries.'

At this juncture Harden threw himself back into his chair and clapped his hands joyously.

'Mr Holmes, I see now that there is nothing within Dr Watson's accounts of your work that exaggerates your powers. You are correct on every count, although

I cannot, for the life of me, understand how you could possibly have identified the name of my company merely from a set of initials.'

No doubt fuelled by the enthusiasm of our client, Holmes was now clearly warming to his task. He suppressed a mischievous smile and lowered his voice as if he was about to divulge a most singular secret.

'Mr Harden, I must inform you that my friend, Dr Watson, read of you in a recent morning paper and he passed this information on to me, but a moment before your arrival!' Harden appeared to be both surprised and disappointed by Holmes' confession, a fact that did not go unnoticed by my friend.

He clapped his hands repeatedly and laughed uproariously, although Harden and I were somewhat slower in reacting in this way.

'I fear that if I continue to betray my secrets in this way, any reputation that I might have accrued will disappear in a thrice!' Holmes' amusement slowly subsided and he soon turned towards

Harden with a steely intent.

'Mr Harden, as gratifying as this brief interlude has been, we have surely wasted enough valuable time by examining this commonplace trivia!'

Harden drained the remains from his coffee cup before clearing his throat. He looked anxiously towards me, for affirmation that he should now begin to recount his problem to us. I raised my pencil and smiled at him reassuringly.

'Thank you. I assure you, gentlemen, that I shall put this matter before you both with as much brevity and accuracy as I can.' Holmes smiled gratefully at Harden when he heard this declaration.

'As Dr Watson so correctly pointed out, I am indeed John Vincent Harden and I have been, until very recently, the most successful tobacco tycoon that this country has ever produced.

'Despite my success and the inevitable wealth that I have accumulated, I have always lived a most frugal and abstemious existence. My wife Claudia and I remain childless to this day and we have lived in a modest town house in Chester Square

26

these past twenty years, with barely a handful of servants.'

'A most humble existence, indeed,' Holmes stated quietly, with an understandable sarcasm, for the fine town houses of Chester Square are among the most sought-after residences in one of the better parts of Belgravia.

Harden chose to ignore Holmes' irony and pulled out his cigar case, which he proceeded to offer around. Holmes and I declined in turn.

'Although they are undoubtedly most fine, I find my cherry wood pipe to be more conducive at the outset of a case,' Holmes explained.

Harden removed the tip from a huge Havana and smiled long and indulgently while he slowly brought it to light. He waved a huge cloud of smoke away from his face before continuing.

'Throughout that time my daily routine had barely altered. My company had its main office in the City and we kept our accounting department in somewhat smaller premises at West Hampstead. I liked to visit both of them on a regular basis and often travelled from my club, which is situated just behind Gower Street, to West Hampstead via the Metropolitan. As you so correctly deduced Mr Holmes, I became a most regular passenger and barely a day went by that did not find me within one of its trains.'

'Excuse me Mr Harden, but surely for a man in your position, a carriage would unquestionably prove to be a more agreeable proposition?' I found myself asking.

'We do keep a small brougham, Dr Watson, but I find the running costs to be prohibitive and I reserve it for those rare occasions when I escort my wife to a social engagement and the like.'

Just then I noticed Holmes eyeing our guest a good deal more quizzically and he ran his finger around the rim of the old man's hat.

'This layer of soot on your hat is still quite fresh!' Holmes stated with some emphasis.

Harden drew on his cigar and viewed my friend with some confusion.

'You appear to be making a point, Mr Holmes, but I fail to see what it might be.'

'Surely now that you have retired there is no real need for you to travel to West Hampstead and subject yourself to the grime and discomfort of the underground railway?'

'Although I am retired, the company is still in full operation and the accountant has requested my assistance in executing the transition of ownership. The work is almost complete and in any event, it only occupies two or three hours of my time each day. Once everything has been signed over, Claudia and I intend to travel extensively for the first time in nearly twenty years!' Harden declared joyfully.

'Mr Harden, with your life seemingly in such fine order, I fail to see what prompted you to seek my consultation with such urgency.' Inexplicably Holmes was taking an obvious dislike to the elderly tobacco baron and he seemed intent on drawing matters towards a speedy conclusion. He tapped out his pipe against the side of the fireplace, lit a cigarette in its place and turned away from Harden to face the window.

'Oh Mr Holmes, do not turn away from me at such a time, for I am being hounded and persecuted to the point where I am at my wits' end!' Harden suddenly exclaimed while clambering back up to his feet.

'Steady your nerves, Mr Harden, steady your nerves — 'persecution' is a most unusual turn of phrase. You do not appear to be maltreated, so explain to me in what manner you have been interfered with,' Holmes suggested while striding back towards the centre of the room.

'It began harmlessly enough, indeed the unusual incidents were so slight and commonplace that individually they were hardly worthy of note and might have even be put down to my own ineptness. Accumulatively, however, they became quite tiresome and over a period of time, a cause of great concern.'

'To what type of incident are you referring and over what period of time would this be?' Holmes asked grudgingly.

Harden returned to his seat and

appeared to be most put out when Holmes applied more concentration to the task of scraping out the bowl of his pipe than he did to the account of this unusual problem.

'Initially, when various items that I use on a regular basis, such as my umbrella for example, began to disappear, I put it down to an oversight on my part. However, I soon realized that another hand was at play, especially when these items suddenly turned up again, but in the most inexplicable of places. For example, a silver-plated trophy, which I had won for playing golf many years ago, suddenly reappeared in the coal cellar!

'The first incident occurred over four months ago, but it has only been over the past fortnight that I have actually been plagued beyond the four walls of my house.' It was only now that Holmes ceased his incessant scraping and turned his attention towards our visitor once more, his eyes gleaming!

'As I explained earlier, for reasons of prudence and convenience, I have become a regular user of the Metropolitan Railway. I travel between Gower Street and West Hampstead stations during the course of the same schedule every day. Consequently, I have become used to seeing some very familiar faces occupying the seats very close to my own, every time that I step upon the train.

'It has only been of late, however, that I have found myself drawing some undesirable and intimidating attention. I am constantly being stared at and sometimes in a most threatening manner. However, my stalkers never seem to be the same person on the following day. They occupy the same seat as each other, they even present an identical pose and menacing demeanour — however, I have never seen any of them more than once. It is almost as if I have somehow become the victim of a gigantic and inexplicable conspiracy!' At this juncture Harden became understandably agitated and he reached into his jacket pocket for his vesta box.

'Although they now appear to be different to each other, do you recognize any of these conspirators as being amongst your fellow passengers from the time before your persecution began?' Holmes asked.

Harden thought long and hard before shaking his head and answering in the negative.

'Are there any obvious visual similarities between any of them, say their age or build, for example?'

'No, not at all and that is the thing that is most damnably strange about the whole business! One day it might be a middle-aged lady, the next a dapper businessman and the next a pretty young nanny. The only thing that they all seem to share is an unwarranted and disturbing obsession with me.'

'Yet you still persist in making this journey despite the discomfort that this strange behaviour is causing you?' I decided to ask.

'Yes Doctor, I did not see why my daily routine should alter; just because a disparate group of characters have decided that I make an interesting subject for their scrutiny.'

'However, that situation has now changed for the worse, and quite recently, I think,' Holmes proposed. Then he added, in answer to our questioning glances, 'Why else would you come to me, after all this time, unless you now feel that you have come under some kind of threat?'

'You are quite correct, Mr Holmes, events have certainly moved in another direction of late. My tormentors are now no longer content to merely stare intently towards me; they have started to talk to me, from under their breath and making contact of quite an aggressive nature. A whispered threat to my life, a clumsy elbow to my rib cage, these are just two of the most recent examples of their outrageous behaviour.

'As you might suppose, I took the matter up with the police, but as no crime has actually been committed, there is very little action that they can take. So I now turn to you, Mr Holmes, in the hope that you might explain to me what this strange persecution can possibly mean. Do you think that my life might actually be in jeopardy?'

Holmes thought long and hard before making his pronouncement and he pursed his lips with pressure from his right forefinger. He cast Harden an oblique and anxious glance, before slowly replying.

'You must be strong, Mr Harden, but I think it to be not unlikely. Do you believe that the most singular occurrences in your home are in some way connected to the more threatening behaviour of your fellow passengers? After all, the disappearance of your personal possessions could only be attributed to your servants and family and you would surely be able to identify them were they to suddenly join you on the Metropolitan.'

'Our servants have been with us for many years, Mr Holmes and I cannot, for one minute, believe that they would collude with those scoundrels on the train. I have recognized nobody from my household during my journeys, of that I am certain.'

'In that case, I suppose that it has not occurred to you that your wife might be behind the temporary misplacement of your cherished objects, as some form of practical joke perhaps?' Holmes suggested mischievously.

'Absolutely not Mr Holmes, indeed I find the very idea totally preposterous and not a little insulting!' Harden protested while rising to his feet again. Undaunted, however, Holmes persisted with this line of questioning.

'Mr Harden, what other reasonable conclusion is one to draw? Given that you trust your servants so implicitly, no one from outside of your household is likely to have run the risk of breaking and entering merely to move a golf trophy from one place to the next! If you cannot see that, perhaps you have formulated a theory of your own that might explain your persecution on the trains?'

'Mr Holmes, that is precisely why I have come here today, to seek your advice. Is there none that you can give me?' Harden asked pleadingly.

'Only that it would be in your best interest were you to start telling me the truth!' With that, Holmes turned away from him once more and disdainfully waved in the direction of the door. — Harden stamped down his foot in rage and stood up as if to leave.

'Well I never, Mr Holmes, I am not used to being spoken to in such a fashion. If you are not able to help me, then I am certain that I shall find someone, of similar ilk, who is both willing and able to.' Harden turned on his heels and slammed our door behind him with a resounding crash. The door onto Baker Street was dealt with in a similar fashion a moment later.

'Well I must say, Holmes, that your dismissal of a potentially intriguing case in such a cavalier fashion goes somewhat against the grain! Are you so certain that Harden has been withholding the truth from you deliberately?'

'Of that, Watson, I am in no doubt. While I am not suggesting for an instant that Harden's story is a complete fabrication, there are certain aspects of his statement that simply do not hold water. The fact that he is so reluctant to reveal them to me suggests that he has been guilty of an indiscretion so shameful that he cannot bring himself to declare it to me.

'Nevertheless, there are certain aspects of this case that are unique in my experience and Mr John Vincent Harden has nowhere else to turn. He will come back before too long, of that you may be assured. In the meantime, Watson, there is nothing to prevent us from making a few inquiries of our own, in the hope that we can put together the pieces of this puzzle before the next stage of Harden's persecution is revealed.'

'Why are you so convinced that Harden has been withholding the truth? I did not see anything in his manner that would have suggested that to you.'

'I am familiar with West Hampstead and I can assure you Watson, that there is no accountancy in that vicinity capable of handling a client as considerable as Harden Tobacco Industries. Furthermore, a company of that scale would undoubtedly incorporate an accounts department within its own head office, so I rejected that notion from the outset.

'I was equally dismissive of the suggestion that Harden would subject himself to the tribulations of the underground railway merely to save a few pounds, when he had already confessed to having a perfectly good brougham at home at his constant beck and call. I would suggest that there lies a far more tempting reason that would induce Harden into making that journey.'

'Well for one thing, there is less chance of his own household discovering his whereabouts by his using the underground service. After all, if he is perpetrating an indiscretion, there is little point in his advertising that fact to his driver and footman!' I suggested.

'Excellent Watson, they were my thoughts exactly! Although, of course, I had the added advantage of having noticed the corner of a lady's handkerchief protruding from Harden's inside pocket, when he reached inside for his cigar case. It had been badly stained with make-up and bore the initials *S.S.*, not *C.H.* as one would expect.' With that, Holmes dashed into his room and reappeared a moment later wearing his coat, a muffler and bearing his small bag and cane.

'Holmes, are we to assume that the next phase of Harden's persecution might involve a threat to his life?' I asked before Holmes had reached the door.

'As you surely know by now, Watson, I never assume. However, it would be a grave folly were we to exclude all possibilities, no matter how unlikely they might seem to be. There is not a moment to lose!'

'Where are you off to?' I asked while remaining firmly rooted to the spot.

'Why to Gower Street, of course, in the hope that Gunner King and his cohorts might aid me in ascertaining the true course of Harden's daily routines and perhaps the identity of the mysterious lady who is now missing one handkerchief.'

I should point out that King was, without a doubt, the finest cabbie in London and his vast knowledge and fortitude had proved to be invaluable to Holmes on many such occasions.

'Holmes, would you like me to travel to West Hampstead? Who knows, Harden's final destination might prove to be every bit as important as his starting point.'

Holmes appeared to be genuinely appreciative of my suggestion.

'Oh Watson, if you would not mind. Ultimately it might prove to be a thankless task, but the time that it might save me could prove to be of immeasurable assistance.' With that Holmes was through the door and he departed from 221b with a cursory call to Mrs Hudson as he slammed the front door behind him.

My own departure was no less urgent than that of Holmes and I hurtled towards Baker Street station while still fastening my heavy overcoat. I decided to forsake the relative speed and comfort of a cab in favour of taking the very same journey as had our beleaguered former client.

During the course of that long and uncomfortable journey, I inquired of the guard to see if he could recognize my description of Harden, but I was greeted with a look of bewilderment and a deliberate shaking of the head. Consequently, I arrived upon the cold, windswept platform of West Hampstead station, with only the ticket clerk to turn to for a clue.

The worthy in question proved to be a genial old man, whose speech and deportment told of better times, long since past. Fortunately his small office proved to be the warmest part of the station and I gratefully accepted his invitation to step inside. Like a good many in his position, the clerk seemed grateful of the opportunity to strike up a conversation and I had to endure a tepid cup of tea and a series of mind-numbing anecdotes, before he finally responded to my initial inquiry.

My patience and endurance were finally to be rewarded. As it turned out, the locals were rather proud of the fact that they had, from amongst their midst, something of a celebrity; an aspiring young actress who went by the stage name of Sophie Sinclair. I did not need reminding of the significance of her initials, but my enthusiasm was dampened by the fact that the clerk had only seen Miss Sinclair in the company of an elderly gentleman but once. I apologized for leaving my teacup three-quarters full and with a grateful hand shake, I took my leave.

I stepped outside to light a cigarette and gazed up at the front of the station. It was a surprisingly small and innocuous façade, fashioned from red brick with only a single arch and it was cradled within a small clutch of run-down shops. At that moment a thin veil of sleet was suddenly whipped into a frenetic dance by the remorseless autumnal wind. I pulled up my collar, pulled down my hat and made my way towards a small alehouse on the opposite side of the road.

On more than one occasion, Holmes had gained valuable information from the loosened tongues of the clients of a public house and therefore I decided to take a leaf out of his book and I stepped inside. In all honesty, it was also an act of self-preservation.

Once I had purchased a large whiskey

from the bar keep, I immediately made my way towards a diminishing fire that was struggling, in vain, to warm that small and dismal hostelry. I stood with my back to the flame so that I could survey my fellow clients and then decide who I should best approach for information. I must confess that my brief appraisal proved to be a disappointment.

I was one of only six who had ventured over the threshold that day and two of these had clearly sampled the landlord's wares to a point beyond all reason! The remainder comprised of two elderly gentlemen engaged in a heated political debate, a young artisan fallen upon hard times and a bucolic ruffian who was mumbling to himself while he drained his tankard of its last drop of ale.

Although he was the closest to me, I forsook the pleasure of conversing with the ruffian and instead made my way towards the artisan. To my dismay, as I turned away from him, I felt the ruffian's hand land upon my shoulder with vigorous intent.

'I say sir!' I protested while I removed

myself from his grasp. His straggly grey hair was as overgrown as was his beer-stained moustache and his overcoat was worn beyond the point of redemption. When he spoke, the stench of beer and tobacco was overwhelming and each word was framed by a stream of bronchial phlegm.

''Ere guv, I meant no 'arm, but I find myself short of the price of tobacco. Could a gent like yourself spare me that?' Each word seemed to be punctuated by a cough so severe that I was forced to cover my mouth with a handkerchief.

'Sir, from the sound of it, more tobacco is the very last thing that you require!' I was on the point of vacating that ghastly place, when the fellow's voice suddenly modulated and dropped to a whisper. I was staggered by this dramatic alteration and stopped dead in my tracks. I turned back and immediately recognized a familiar smile breaking through the bedraggled hair.

'Watson, do not betray a single indication of recognition, I beseech you. Now give me one of your cigarettes and I

shall meet you outside in five minutes.'
Even from within this startling disguise,
Holmes' instructions had their usual
compliant effect upon me. I handed over
the cigarette without hesitation and I
stepped out onto the windswept street
once more.

I paced back and forth in agitation for
a minute or two until Holmes' ruffian, as
good as his word, shuffled through the ale
house door and lurched towards me
aggressively. Holmes remained in character until we had turned a corner and he
was certain that we could not be spied
upon. He led me towards the cab of
Gunner King and it was only once we
were safely on board and moving towards
town once more that Holmes slowly
began to remove his disguise.

By the time that he had removed the
last tuft of hair and straightened his frock
coat, Holmes' ruffian had all but drifted
from memory and I was left with my old
friend once more and a string of
questions. Holmes could not help but
laugh at my nonplussed demeanour, but
he allayed my interrogation by raising his

hand up while he lit the cigarette that I had given him and took down the soothing smoke. He ran his fingers through his hair and bore the expression of a boy who had just been presented with his most sought-after gift.

'Oh Watson, before you ask I must tell you that I arrived here ahead of you because King tore up the streets of London while you were meandering along on the train. As commendable as your choice of transport undoubtedly was, you were sadly ignorant of the need for speed. As soon as King had confirmed my worst fears, I donned the persona that you have just witnessed and rushed to meet you here before it was too late.'

Holmes' breathless explanation had done little to make the thing any clearer to me, so I shook my head slowly and told him so.

'In truth, Watson, for once I would have been surprised had you been able to grasp the situation. Events have unfolded at such a rate, that even I am not yet clear on one or two details! However, we have a little time before we arrive back at Baker

Street, so it would only be right were I to pass on my limited knowledge of the matter to you.

'No sooner had I mentioned the address in Chester Square, than King and his colleagues were able to put together a schedule of Harden's movements in a very short space of time. To avoid detection, Harden hailed his cabs from nearby Eaton Square. Although he did indeed visit his company's offices in the City, he rarely remained there for any length of time and he spent the majority of his days within his club in Pall Mall.

'I knew that my knowledge of London had not become so shabby that I could not recognize Harden's assertion that his club was near Gower Street as anything other than a lie. There is no such establishment, I assure you, Watson. Quite often he would divert his journey to Gower Street via the Garrick Theatre, where his vehicle would await the arrival of a vivacious young actress who goes by the name of . . . '

'Sophie Sinclair!' I declared triumphantly. For once I had truly stopped

Sherlock Holmes in his tracks. He sat there, as if dumbstruck, for a moment or two, before turning towards me, smiling proudly.

'How could you possibly have known that?' he asked incredulously.

I explained to Holmes the outcome of my visit with the ticket clerk and the reasons for my subsequent visit to the alehouse.

'Well, well, well . . . it would seem that our two diverse journeys have culminated in the same location having reached the same conclusions,' Holmes stated just as we had turned the corner into Baker Street. 'Well done, King!' Holmes called up to the driver as we pulled up outside 221b.

As we let ourselves in, I asked, 'I still do not see how you also ended up in that same ghastly place, moreover in that astounding disguise.'

'I discovered that on those days when Harden forsook the pleasures of the theatre, he and Miss Sinclair would use that dubious establishment as their point of rendezvous. Obviously I could not visit that place in my own person, for fear of detection. Harden would have recognized me in a thrice.'

'Of course, but are you any closer to discovering the source of Harden's persecution?' I asked as we reached the top landing.

'I will only be able to determine that once I have discovered the true nature of Harden's relationship with Sophie Sinclair. That information I expect to receive from Harden himself when he returns here tomorrow — after all, by that time he will have had all night during which to cool his heels. Good night, old fellow.'

I was grateful for an early night as I made my way, with a slow determination, upstairs to my room.

To my surprise, Holmes was still in his room when I came downstairs the following morning. Although he was prone to keeping the most bohemian of hours at times, he was normally highly energized when active upon a case and I had expected to see him at his morning cup of coffee. I took advantage of his absence by having the first read of the papers. The lead headline of The Times sent me scurrying towards Holmes' room in a state of great agitation.

When he did not respond to my hammering upon his door, I took the unprecedented step of entering without invitation and I began to shake him by the shoulder. This was a treatment that I had received at Holmes' hand, on many similar occasions down the years. However, now that the roles were being reversed, I did so with much trepidation as I could not be sure of his reaction. I decided to present him with the headline as soon as his eyes were focussed, in the certain knowledge that its contents would deflect any anger that he might otherwise have felt towards me.

Holmes was clearly shaken to the core by the awful news and he was out of his bed and at his toilet in an instant.

TOBACCO BARON HAS FATAL FALL

While Holmes completed his preparations, I looked back over this dramatic headline and studied the scant details of the death of John Vincent Harden that were printed below. According to the initial reports, Harden was seen being backed up towards the edge of the platform at West Hampstead station, by the aggressive behaviour of two women who were clearly much disturbed. One of these women seemed to push him in the chest and as a consequence, Harden fell headlong on to the track in front of an oncoming train. His death had been both gruesome and instantaneous.

At such an early stage of the inquiry, neither of the women had been identified as yet and the younger of the two had disappeared prior to the arrival of the authorities. Our old friend, Inspector Lestrade of Scotland Yard, was in charge of the investigation and he had decided to hold the older of the two women for further questioning.

Holmes was ready in a thrice and while our cab was speeding towards West Hampstead, I read out the brief report that I have just described. Holmes sat silently and thoughtfully for a moment or two, before peering at me with remorse set deep within his troubled eyes.

'Oh Watson, I fear that I am guilty of having seriously misjudged the gravity of the next stage of Harden's persecution,' he said quietly.

'Or perhaps Harden's death was a direct result of nothing more than misadventure?' I suggested in the hope of alleviating my friend's dark regret.

Holmes slowly nodded his head with a weak but hopeful smile.

We sat in silence for the remainder of the journey and we were met at the station entrance by the sight of the brazen and weasel-like features of our old friend, Inspector Lestrade, who appeared to be in a most animated disposition.

'Well, well, Mr Holmes, I had not expected to see you here today and that is for sure. I suppose that you already have some knowledge of the matter, which you have absolutely no intention of withholding from me?' Lestrade sarcastically suggested.

'I have become acquainted with certain facts that may help to clarify this tragic situation and I will gladly share with you any data that might prove to be relevant. Firstly, however, we must learn what we may from the trackside, if the area has not been too heavily trafficked in the meantime.'

'I assure you, Mr Holmes, that there is very little to show you there. The decimated and grisly remains of Mr Harden have long since been removed and his wife, whom I strongly suspect to be his murderer, is safely within my custody for further questioning,' Lestrade responded, with understandable apprehension. All too often in the past, the enthusiastic inspector had believed himself to be upon the right path to solving a case, only to find that my friend was already one step ahead of him.

'Nevertheless, I would like to judge that for myself, with your kind permission, of course.' Holmes' smile was anything but engaging and Lestrade waved him towards the site of the tragedy with an air of resignation. Before he began his examination of the area indicated, Holmes gave me his permission to explain every aspect of our involvement to the bewildered detective.

While I was making my report, I noticed Holmes hurl himself down upon his stomach on an area of the platform that appeared to be dangerously close to the track. He pulled out his glass and examined the spot where Harden had evidently lost his balance, for it was marked with a small white cross of chalk. He then wriggled away from the edge of the platform, no doubt tracing Harden's progress in reverse.

Holmes stood up sharply and dusted himself down thoroughly, before asking Lestrade to briefly explain the facts that had led him to his conclusions. Lestrade was only too happy to oblige.

As it transpired, he was able to add very little to the brief accounts that we had seen in the morning papers. Lestrade had obtained three eyewitness accounts that seemed to verify his suspicions, including that of my old friend the ticket clerk. They all confirmed that two women had begun to berate the hapless Harden in unison and he had edged away from them in a state of considerable alarm. The older of the two women seemed to reach out towards him and it was at that moment that Harden stumbled in front of the train, resulting in his horrific demise.

'Although the younger of the women made away long before we could reach the scene, Mrs Harden was evidently too shaken and stunned by the results of her actions to do likewise and she awaited our arrival in the ticket office, as if resigned to her fate. Naturally, it did not take me long to put two and two together and Mrs Harden seemed to confess to her crime while she was being led away by my constables.' Lestrade crossed his arms smugly and his knowing smile indicated that he now believed Holmes' intervention to be redundant.

'She seemed to confess to her crimes, Inspector? That is certainly an unusual turn of phrase. Is it not just as likely that her state of mind prevented her from putting any cohesive thoughts together that might have stood in her defence?' Holmes suggested.

'That is mere speculation on your part, Mr Holmes, but even were it to be true that would still not negate the testimony of those witnesses.' Lestrade seemed to be determined to stand his ground on this occasion.

'Ah, but I am sure that you would not be averse to me demonstrating an alternative explanation, were it to lead us to the truth. Eyewitnesses can only account for what they believe that they might have seen,' Holmes persisted.

'We all want to arrive at the truth, Mr Holmes, but I can assure you of the witnesses' reliability.'

Holmes chose to ignore Lestrade's last remark and instead he strode over to the unsheltered section of the platform where the sleet was still hitting the ground. He shuffled his feet around in the puddles until he seemed satisfied that his heels and soles were thoroughly dampened and then returned to where Lestrade and I were awaiting his return. We were both amused and perplexed by Holmes' inexplicable actions and when he began to slowly count out a few steps while moving backwards, we were no less confused.

Finally when he pulled up at a safe distance from the edge of the platform, he beckoned me over to him.

'Now, push me in the chest, Watson, but please make allowance for the strength of an elderly lady.'

Naturally I carried out Holmes' bidding and then looked on helplessly as he stumbled back slightly before he took to the floor again with his glass. Once he appeared to be satisfied with the results of his examination, he invited Lestrade and I to join him.

'Obviously this first line of muddied prints belonged to the late Mr Harden and they were formed while he backed away from his persecutors. As you can see they are spaced out equally, but more significantly, they continue right up to the very edge of the platform. My prints, on the other hand, although following a parallel line to those of Harden, suddenly break off at the point when Watson pushed me in the chest. See how that slight but sudden movement caused my shoes to create skid marks both here and here.

'You know, it never ceases to amaze me, Inspector, how sceptical and confused you appear to be at some of my more unpredictable actions. Have I not assured you, on numerous occasions, that there is a perfectly sound and logical reason behind everything that I do?'

'That is all very well, Mr Holmes, but I am still not convinced that your very fine demonstration devalues the testimony that I have already taken,' Lestrade protested, but without any real conviction.

'In that case, perhaps you might be persuaded were I to produce an alternative witness who might be willing to confirm my findings?'

'I am not aware of any outstanding witness. To whom might you be referring?'

'Why, I am referring to none other than Sophie Sinclair, who happens to be the second lady to have harangued Harden on the platform. I am certain that a local celebrity such as she will not be too difficult to locate in such a small community.'

'Oh no, Mr Holmes, I am afraid that you have missed the mark this time. She was seen bolting from the station at the very moment of Harden's fatal fall. She will be long gone by now!'

'Indulge me for a mere ten minutes, Inspector, and I shall produce her for you.'

Holmes was as good as his word and before long we three found ourselves outside the front door to a small suite of rooms above the local hardware shop.

The door was opened by an absolutely charming young woman, who greeted us with a resigned and philosophical smile. She was tall and slim and her long, dark hair was curled luxuriantly. She did not pause to ask us for our identities or our reasons for coming to her door, but moved inside and invited us into her small, but artistically appointed sitting room. Lestrade and I produced our notebooks and pencils, while Holmes paced around upon the extremely limited floor space. Miss Sinclair allowed us no chance to speak.

'Gentlemen, I know precisely why you

are here and at the outset, please allow me to request that you should not prejudge me.'

'That is not our intention, Miss Sinclair; we merely wish to discover the truth,' I replied gently.

'That is no easy thing to do, Dr Watson.' She smiled exquisitely.

'So you know me then?' I asked.

'I know of both you and Mr Sherlock Holmes from the most vivid descriptions that are contained within your stirring accounts.'

Holmes grunted impatiently during our exchange of pleasantries and he lit a cigarette by the open window. Miss Sinclair hurriedly began her story.

'I have asked you not to judge me because in the very recent past, ladies who took to the stage accrued a certain kind of reputation, if you take my meaning.' We all nodded our confirmation, although with an air of embarrassment.

'I assure you gentlemen that I received a decent education and I was, therefore, resolved to making my living in serious theatre. In recent months I have been fortunate enough to be offered minor roles in works by Shakespeare, Shaw and the like and gradually I am gaining a most positive reputation.

'I first met John Harden when he arrived backstage to congratulate me after a performance of *The Merry Wives of Windsor*. He presented me with a magnificent bouquet of roses and dramatically extolled the virtues of my performance. Despite his age, he had retained a winning charm and I found myself being quite swept off my feet by his compliments and enthusiasm. I allowed him to escort me to the very finest restaurants and before too long our trysts become quite a regular occurrence.'

Holmes turned towards her suddenly and addressed her in a tone that I considered to be quite unwarranted.

'Did you not find the clandestine nature of your rendezvous in any way suspicious? After all, to arrange meetings at a disreputable public house or to forsake a fine carriage for the underground railway was hardly the behaviour of a man of honour.'

Miss Sinclair appeared to have been undaunted by Holmes' judgemental attitude and I was strangely proud of her for refusing to lower her eyes from his.

'Mr Holmes, I am not a naïve young girl nor am I a fool! I had no doubt that he was a married man but for so long as his intentions and behaviour towards me remained honourable I did not feel as if we were doing any real harm. He assured me that his wife had ceased to have any interest in his comings and goings a long time ago and that I was the only person who had ever captivated him in such a way.

'However, it soon became apparent that every word of his had been a complete lie. I had a chance encounter with an old friend of mine from my early years upon the stage who had fallen upon hard times. Adele Fox had recoiled in horror when I told her of my relationship with Mr Harden. She had had a similar experience with him, but a few months previously and she told me how he had forced himself upon her on many occasions, something that she had to use considerable force to rebuff!

'At once I was resolved to bringing things to an immediate conclusion. After all, if he had lied about one thing or the other, how was I to know of the immeasurable grief that our trysts may have been causing his wife? When I told Harden of my decision his rage was something that I would hope never to have to experience again. He turned bright red, yelled obscenities at me at the top of his voice and threatened to destroy my career by using unspeakable methods.'

'The man was an absolute black-guard!' I exclaimed. I noticed that her recollections were causing Miss Sinclair considerable distress and I immediately offered her my handkerchief, which she accepted with a gracious smile. After a moment's pause, she continued.

'He stormed out of my rooms and left me with his threats still echoing around my head and I shuddered at the thought of having allowed a creature such as he within my home. I was resolved to informing his wife of his despicable behaviour, in the hope that we both might have our revenge. I donned a disguise, which I was well able to obtain from the theatre's wardrobe and make-up departments and arrived at Chester Square once I was certain of Harden's absence for the day.

'To my surprise and immense relief, Mrs Harden was well aware of her husband's dalliances and rather than unleashing her wrath upon me, she even agreed to contribute to my conspiracy! It was agreed that she would do everything she could to unsettle him at home while colleagues of mine would confound him every time he boarded his train. He was so resolved to winning me back that he bombarded me with gifts and messages from every angle.

'I am certain that this was to satisfy his ego rather than an expression of any real affection that he professed to have had for me. I rebuffed every effort of his and each visit to my rooms was met with a closed and bolted door. The encounters that were distressing him on the train were gradually being intensified by design and he was clearly becoming affected by our persecution.

'Finally, before matters got out of hand, I agreed to meet him upon the platform at West Hampstead station. I informed Mrs Harden of my intention and she agreed to meet me there so that the three of us might reach a resolution. Sadly, that was never meant to be. He extended his rage and insults to the two of us and we moved towards him to silence him in so public a place. You know the tragic outcome of our efforts and Mrs Harden even tried to pull him back before he reached his sorry end.'

'So he was not pushed?' Unbelievably, there was a trace of regret in Lestrade's voice when he asked this redundant question.

'Mrs Claudia Harden is a kind and gentle soul who deserved someone far better than John Vincent Harden!' Miss Sinclair declared with much sincerity.

Holmes was already making his way towards the front door and Sophie Sinclair graciously showed us out.

'Once again, Mr Holmes, you have saved a potential victim of my own

ineptitude from the direst of consequences! Mrs Harden and I have much to
be grateful to you for,' Lestrade admitted
while we went in search of a cab.

'No, not at all, Inspector, you are
merely guilty of reaching your conclusions far too quickly and easily. A simple
adjustment to your report will show that
Mrs Harden was retained in your custody
merely to allow her time to recover from
the shock of seeing her beloved husband's
tragic death, well away from the public
gaze.'

Lestrade nodded his gratitude and we
continued our journey back to Baker
Street in a contemplative silence. I was
in little doubt that the Harden affair
would do nothing to dispel my friend's
well-documented misogynistic nature.
However, I did not share Holmes'
mistrust of the fairer sex and I was
resolved to attending a performance at
the Garrick Theatre in the not too
distant future.

By the time that we had reached Baker
Street and watched Lestrade disappear
around the corner in the cab, my mind

had taken a different train of thought. Was it not possible that Harden's club in Pall Mall was none other than the Diogenes Club, of recent dubious repute? Furthermore, why had that thought not also occurred to Holmes, or if it had, why had he not aired it to me?

Nevertheless, by the time that I had reached my room, my thoughts had once again returned to the delightful Sophie Sinclair!

2

The Egyptian Gargoyle

Despite the exhausting nature of the previous day's adventures, I found myself awake and alert long before the remainder of the household had arisen. My thoughts of the night before had turned in an entirely different direction by the morning and once I was shaved and dressed, I was a little disappointed to note that Mrs Hudson was not yet in her kitchen. I shrugged off the notion of waking her with a rap on her door and decided instead to extend my walk beyond the news vendor's stand.

The air was fresh and invigorating and the streets were pleasantly free of traffic at this early hour. Before too long, I found myself in the park and I spread out my paper upon a bench while I smoked my first pipe of the day. By the time I had finished it, and the majority of the paper,

I felt certain that my breakfast would be awaiting me upon my return to Baker Street. I rubbed my hands together in anticipation as I closed the door behind me and the aromas from the kitchen added fuel to my hunger. Consequently, I am certain that my frustration upon finding Holmes deep in conversation with a total stranger might be well understood.

It was unusual to find my friend dressed and attentive at this early hour and I could not be certain as to whether the stranger was a client and not a private visitor for Holmes. Therefore, I began to retrace my steps and I mumbled a quiet apology. Holmes was up on his feet in an instant and he ushered me over to my regular chair with a disarming urgency.

'Watson, allow me to introduce you to Mr Denbigh Grey! Mr Grey, my friend and colleague Dr Watson, before whom you may speak as freely as you can before me. Oh Watson, you will stay to take notes?' Holmes asked anxiously when he saw me climb out of my chair once more.

'I shall just get my notebook and pencil.' I smiled reassuringly.

'Excellent, perhaps you would also be so good as to ask Mrs Hudson for a tray of coffee, on your way back?' I baulked at this notion, for the smells from the kitchen were still playing havoc with my senses!

Nevertheless, by the time that the coffee things had been removed and Mrs Hudson had finished complaining about her spoiled meal, I was fully engaged upon the matter at hand, with my pencil at the ready.

Mr Denbigh Grey was certainly a nervous little person. I would wager that he stood at little more than 5ft 2in and he also suffered from the additional disadvantage of being unusually slight and fragile in appearance. His face was grey and sallow and his strained eyes and the magnitude of his spectacle lenses told of endless hours of intense study. He had on a worn, albeit well tailored, grey suit and the small black moustache, which was perched precariously above pale, thin lips, was constantly twitching back and forth in apprehension.

Sherlock Holmes was certainly not

insensible to Grey's circumstance and he responded with his most charming smile.

'Mr Grey, although you had already hinted at the cause of your anxiety prior to Watson's timely return, it would be of immeasurable benefit to both of us were you to recount the exact circumstances that have led you to our door. Obviously you were a rather successful teacher, at some point in your career; however you have now fallen on hard times and eke out a meagre living in a somewhat less advantageous form of employ, probably translation.'

I realized that on this occasion Holmes had not deliberately displayed his gifts as a means to impress his client, but more to calm and reassure him. I decided to save Holmes the irksome task of having to explain his observation and I noted that he was otherwise engaged in the task of chiselling out the bowl of his pipe with the sharp end of a twisted compass.

'Your briefcase is of a type most commonly used by teachers and although it is of the finest quality, its worn and battered appearance indicates that you are no longer able to renew it. Equally your suit has clearly seen better days and the elbow patches indicate hours of intense study hunched over books. The sheets of paper that are protruding from the top of your case are written in ancient Greek.'

'That is most excellent work Watson, it really is. However, I fear that should I divulge any more of my secrets, I shall be redundant in next to no time!' Holmes smiled.

'Gentlemen, sadly you are both correct on every point and it is upon a matter arising from my current profession that I have come to seek your advice and help today.'

'Mr Grey, I assure you that you are very welcome to both. Now please, explain your problem from the very beginning and pray omit nothing, no matter how trivial it might at first appear to you.'

Grey sat very upright on the edge of his chair and he immediately brought out the sheets of paper to which I had just referred.

'As you have both observed, as a rule I am not exactly inundated with work. I have circulated my name at various libraries and certain scholastic institutions and the wide range of languages with which I am proficient ensure I have enough work to keep body and soul together. Usually I am approached by the parents of young students whose charges are struggling with their studies, but my fees are low by necessity and the work infrequent.

'Consequently, you will understand my joy and not a little surprise, when I received a letter the other day requesting my services and offering me a remuneration far in excess of anything that I would ordinarily have conceived of!'

'By any chance, did you retain this auspicious item of correspondence?' Holmes asked.

'Sadly no, but you must understand that at the time I had no conception of its eventual significance. How could I have done?' Grey became quite agitated at the thought of his lack of foresight and he began to remonstrate with himself under his breath. Clearly he spent much of his time in total solitude.

'Do not dwell on this too much, Mr Grey, for I am far more interested in the events that have since led you to appreciate the letter's importance. For example, would you mind divulging the level of payment that was being offered to you?' Holmes asked in a soft and calming tone.

Grey shook his head and began to focus once more upon the matter at hand.

'No indeed, because the level of payment is one of the reasons for my coming to you in the first place. The letter promised me no less than twenty pounds, should I decide to accept the commission and a further twenty pounds upon its completion! As you can imagine, this is considerably in excess of anything I might normally earn in a full calendar month of hard work. All I was required to do, in order to receive this king's ransom, was translate into English a transcript of the campaigns of Alexander the Great from its original Greek. This was a task that I was well able and glad to perform, so I accepted this offer without even a moment's hesitation.'

'So you were suspicious of your employer's motives from the very beginning and yet you still decided to proceed with the undertaking?' Holmes asked accusingly.

'Yes Mr Holmes, however you must understand that a man in my financial predicament is willing to overlook such things if an opportunity to improve matters happens to present itself. I even closed my eyes to the fact that the work was presented to me under circumstances that were unusual, to say the least.'

Holmes arched his eyebrow, lit his pipe and invited Denbigh Grey to continue with an impatient gesture of his right hand.

'Perhaps to refer to the circumstances as being unusual is something of an understatement. In retrospect, I would describe them as being sinister and not a little intimidating. After my client and I had exchanged our initial correspondence, it was agreed that we should meet in a small first floor office in nearby Park

Street. Upon my arrival I was a little put off by the building's neglected exterior, but this feeling increased somewhat once I had gained the upper floor.

'The small office, to which I had been directed, was not only derelict but it had also been cleared of any form of furnishings and fittings. It was fortunate that our meetings had been arranged for during daylight hours, as even the lighting had been ripped out of the crumbling walls! It was clear to me at once that there had been no intention of my ever carrying out the work there and that, for reasons that I could not even begin to fathom, my client intended this room to be nothing more than a point of exchange.

'Why our business could not have been carried out under a more civilized set of circumstances is beyond me, so it was fortunate indeed that we were never there for more than a minute or two on each occasion.'

At this point, Holmes suddenly raised his hand to halt Grey in the middle of his most intriguing narrative.

'Before you continue, Mr Grey, it

would be of great benefit to me if you would describe in precise detail the appearance of your most singular client,' Holmes requested in an apologetic tone.

'To date, I have been to Park Street on two separate occasions and I have been met by a different gentleman each time. They are both of Germanic origin, but I can only describe one of them with any accuracy as the second meeting took place during the early evening and my client's agent was shrouded in the gathering gloom and a large muffler. He was quite stout, as I recall and the only feature that I can describe was a heavy, jet-black moustache that gleamed with wax. He spoke no English at all but he indiscreetly betrayed his name when we exchanged our papers — Carl Irvin — and he behaved with the uncertain hesitancy of a subordinate.'

Holmes and I exchanged shrugs of ignorance, as the name held no significance for either of us.

'The other person, who was undoubtedly the coordinator of this operation, was a most forbidding and singular individual indeed. He too spoke with a Germanic accent but he had a perfect grasp of the English language and he used it to an eloquent and chilling effect. There were no pleasantries exchanged during our initial meeting and he made it clear at once that there would be dire consequences should I betray the discretion and confidences that he insisted upon.

'He stipulated that I would only be entrusted with a small section of the manuscript at a time and he demanded a swift conclusion to the entire matter, despite my protestations that ancient Greek was not exactly my forte! I could not understand why there should be such urgency attached to a task such as this and I became suspicious of his inscrutable motives. However, he would not be put off and his threatening appearance made it difficult for me to deny him.

'Although not a tall man, his sheer physical presence produced an indomitable effect. When he removed his hat he exposed a thick, round head that was bereft of hair, save for an unusual thin red rim than ran around its circumference.

His eyebrows and moustache mirrored that rim and when he removed his monocle, his green piercing eyes chilled me to the bone!'

'He is indeed a most singular and formidable sounding individual,' Holmes remarked, whilst trying his utmost to stifle his excitement. 'Can you recall from which eye he removed the monocle?'

'Oh yes, Mr Holmes, it was his left, of that am I am most certain.'

'In heaven's name, Holmes . . . ' Holmes compelled me to silence with an urgent and impatient wave of his hand, for Denbigh Grey had surely just described our former adversary, Theodore Daxer, the Austrian spy of deadly repute! Therefore, I could not understand Holmes' reluctance to divulge his identity, despite the obvious threat posed to our client by his intimidating employer.

Understandably I shared Holmes' excitement upon hearing this description, for the last time that we had seen Daxer had been at the conclusion of The Dundas Separation Case.[1] His vitriolic threats had been echoing around our heads, while the Kentish police had led him away into custody. Holmes shared my confusion and resentment upon hearing that Daxer had somehow attained an early release and the name of Sir Oswald Austin-Simons QC immediately sprang to my mind. It was he who had arranged the release of the men in brown and he had even represented the deadly Roger Ashley during our investigation into the unholy trinity. Obviously, the confirmation of his involvement in this instance would have to wait for another more appropriate time.

'Mr Grey, as compelling as your story has been thus far, I am certain that there is yet another reason for you seeking my consultation today. After all, the circumstances that have led to your commission have been known to you for some time. Therefore, a further discovery has undoubtedly spurred you to action,' Holmes confidently declared.

Grey hesitated for a moment before responding to Holmes' assertion, while he gathered his thoughts.

'Once again, Mr Holmes, you are

absolutely correct and the other reason for my visit is the most confusing aspect of this whole affair. It is the anomalies, you see. They are so glaringly obvious, even to the most amateur of historians, that there seems to be no reason for concealing them within the text whatsoever!

'The first passage that I discovered bore reference to Alexander's entrance into the ancient Egyptian city of Thebes. There is a description of a magnificent temple, the roof of which is decorated with a series of gargoyle grotesques.'

Grey paused for a moment to allow Holmes and I time to digest the significance of his statement. Although this had not been lost on me, Grey and I were both mildly amused by the look of confusion upon the face of my friend. Holmes had always explained away his ignorance upon certain subjects by extolling the virtues of only storing away facts and knowledge that were pertinent to his own peculiar and unique profession. Consequently, his knowledge of cigarette and cigar ashes, for example, was far more important and relevant to him than the positions of the planets within our solar system. Of course Denbigh Grey was not privy to this aspect of Holmes' nature, so his surprise at having to explain himself further can be well understood.

'Mr Holmes, although the gargoyle itself was not uncommon upon Egyptian temples, the gargoyle grotesque was not introduced until the neo-gothic architects employed them upon churches in medieval times. The description of the temples of Thebes predates them by over a thousand years!'

'Could it not be possible that the original scribe merely made a simple error?' Holmes asked.

Grey slowly shook his head.

'That would not have been possible without a point of reference, but even if it had been, that would still not explain a reference to the Pharaoh Rameses Xll.'

This time my own confusion mirrored that of Holmes and this only served to heighten Grey's surprise and exasperation.

'Gentlemen, there were only eleven pharaohs who bore that name!'

Holmes sprang sharply to his feet with that familiar glint of excitement flashing across his eyes. He pressed his lips with his forefinger and for a moment he appeared to be oblivious to either the presence of Grey or myself, so lost in thought was he. Denbigh Grey had been visibly stunned by Holmes' sudden reactions and he looked to me for guidance, unsure as to whether he should still remain in his seat or beat a hasty retreat. I motioned for him to wait a while longer and sure enough, after little more than three minutes, Holmes turned towards the agitated historian, bearing a suppressed smile of gratification.

'Mr Grey, yours is a most singular little problem, I must say, if not unique in my experience. As things stand at the moment, the reasons for your client's insistence upon secrecy and urgency are inexplicable to me. Although I am reasonably certain that they are not born of a scholastic motive. Have you formulated a theory of your own, by any chance?' Holmes asked with a doubtful smile.

Grey shook his head slowly and disconsolately.

'I am, predominantly, a student of ancient history and it is inconceivable to me that someone would deliberately insert a series of such incongruities into so important a text. My client does not appear to be of a scholarly nature and to be quite frank with you, Mr Holmes, I found his entire demeanour to be quite aggressive and intimidating.

'His desire for discretion was quite explicit however; therefore I reasoned that a consultation with the regular police force was totally out of the question. So I have turned to you, Mr Holmes, in the hope that you might provide me with the guidance that I am so sorely in need of.'

Grey's uncertainty and his total reliance on Holmes' abilities and counsel clearly touched a cord with my friend, whose manner immediately softened towards our client. He placed his hand reassuringly upon Grey's shoulder and returned slowly to his chair. He spent a moment or two in slowly lighting his pipe.

'My first instinct was to advise you to withdraw from your commission without a moment's hesitation. After all, your client's motives are dubious to say the least! However, upon further deliberation, that course of action would also involve its own set of risks. From your description of the man, I would say that he does not sound like the type of individual who would broker refusal in a favourable light and we must bear in mind the fact that he does seem to know how to locate you.

'Therefore, my advice to you would be to follow his instructions to the letter and advise me at once of any further anomalies that you might discover. Are you far into the work?'

'Although I am not familiar with this particular manuscript, my knowledge of the life of Alexander seems to indicate that I am not yet halfway through. Do you think it likely that further discrepancies will reveal themselves to me?' Grey asked.

'I would be very surprised if they did not. Otherwise there would be no reason for your client to continue with the project,' Holmes replied. 'When does he require the next instalment by?'

'I will collect the third section tomorrow evening at the same location, unless, of course, you advise me otherwise, Mr Holmes. I must confess that your use of the word 'risk' has made me feel more than a little uneasy. Will you be able to accompany me?'

Holmes shook his head repeatedly.

'If I was to be observed I fear the risk to you would increase considerably. You would have broken a confidence and thereby become a liability to your employers. As matters stand and while you continue with the work, you will be quite safe, I assure you. In the meantime I will endeavour to unravel this mystery of yours with all speed.' There was something dismissive in Holmes' phrasing and Grey suddenly felt compelled to jump to his feet.

He shook us both fervently by the hand but paused by the door before taking his leave.

'Mr Holmes, despite your assurances, I

fear that there shall be grave conse-quences for me should I complete my work before you have completed yours,' Grey stated gravely.

Holmes did not respond, neither facially nor verbally, but instead went to his room to fetch out his blackboard and chalk.

'Dr Watson will take down your address in order that we might inform you of any fresh developments, as and when they occur. I would ask you to report any fresh anomalies to me within an instant of your discovery.' Holmes dismissed him with a cursory wave before turning to his blackboard.

After I had copied down his address, I led Denbigh Grey to the street door.

'Be assured, Mr Grey, that Mr Holmes will work tirelessly towards bringing this affair to a satisfactory conclusion, long before there is any threat to your good self. Good day to you.' The little man doffed his hat and shuffled off down the street with an urgent speed.

Once I was certain that he was out of earshot, I raced up the stairs to remonstrate with my friend for his flagrant disregard for our client's welfare. After all, he had recognized full well Grey's description of Theodore Daxer and knew as well as I of the despicable acts that Daxer was capable of. As it transpired I might have saved myself the trouble, for Holmes had pre-empted my every word. From my expression he would have known that he was about to receive a verbal assault, so he held up a hand of surrender and deflected my objections with an immediate and undeniable defence.

'Watson, of course I am aware of the potential dangers of allowing Mr Grey's ignorance, but you must understand that I have no other choice! Clearly these anomalies are nothing more than an extremely subtle code. However, I fear that if I am to break this code I will need more clues and I am certain that there are further anomalies within the manuscript for Grey to discover. Daxer will not harm him until his work has been concluded and by then we shall have Daxer's secrets safely within our grasp.'

'You are so certain that you will be able to break this code? After all, we are talking about a man's life.'

Holmes glared at me from under a dark and furrowed brow.

'I am sure that you recall my maxim; that which one man has created another can discover. Therefore, kindly do not disturb me further for the rest of the day . . . not even for food!' Holmes smiled, obviously aware of the fact that the arrival of Denbigh Grey had denied me my customary breakfast. I was on the point of leaving the room when Holmes halted my steps with a brief but ominous warning.

'Before you depart for the kitchen and to satisfy you that I am not taking Mr Grey's life in too light a regard, let me feed you a single thought to chew upon. If Austin-Simons does prove to be responsible for Daxer's early release, you can be assured that once again we shall be swimming through some very dark and turbulent waters.'

Holmes' words had not entirely eradicated my hunger, but I was certainly descending towards the kitchen with far less enthusiasm than I had previously. As I closed the door behind me, the sound of chalk being scratched across the blackboard showed me that Holmes was already hard at work.

3

The Venetian Mandolin

Mrs Hudson had graciously allowed me to take my barely adequate breakfast within her parlour. I had explained to her the nature of Holmes' warning and she threw her arms up in the air in exasperated resignation, before allowing me to share her table.

Leaving our landlady to clear up the clutter, I retraced my steps to the park for a pipe or two and then decided to return to my room to go through some papers that I had brought home with me from my surgery. However, by the time that I had reached the first landing, my curiosity had got the better of me and I decided to defy Holmes' instructions. I opened the door with as much silence and stealth as I could muster with the intention of spying upon Holmes' progress while attempting to evade detection. To my surprise I could hear two familiar voices coming from behind the half-opened door. The more recognizable of the two called out to me with anger and impatience.

'You might just as well join us, Watson, once you have retrieved your invaluable notebook of course!'

I felt embarrassed by my failed deception and I hurried up the stairs to do Holmes' bidding. Upon my return, I discovered that our old friend Inspector Bradstreet was feeling as awkward as I had been at having interrupted Holmes' work at the blackboard. One glance at the scrawled mess showed me that all was not going well thus far and Holmes had evidently broken several pieces of chalk in his frustration.

Holmes had often described Bradstreet as being a dogged yet uninspiring detective, although he had also proved to be a most valuable ally on some of Holmes' more notable cases. His work at the conclusion of the Bruce Partington[1] affair, for example, had subsequently left Holmes feeling duty bound to assist

Bradstreet at every opportunity. He waved me impatiently to my chair.

'Watson, your clumsy arrival has proved to be most timely, for the good inspector was about to explain to me the reason behind his inopportune intrusion.'

Bradstreet had yet to take a seat and he stood awkwardly in the centre of the room with his bowler still firmly in place. He had always cut a solid and resolute figure, yet he appeared to be unusually anxious on this occasion and he was constantly toying with his bullish moustache.

'Mr Holmes, I really cannot apologize enough for this interruption, but I can assure you that I would not have bothered you at all were the matter not of the utmost moment.' Holmes' attitude softened and he smiled as he pushed forward a chair.

'Oh Bradstreet do sit down, you are cluttering up the room, you know. Now explain to me with as much clarity and brevity as you can the reason for your visit here today.' Holmes placed a pointed emphasis upon the word 'brevity'!

Bradstreet placed his hat upon the table and brought out a well-thumbed notebook of his own.

'Gentlemen, you have no doubt heard of that artefact often referred to as the Venetian mandolin?' Bradstreet appeared to be unusually surprised when he observed Holmes and I exchange glances of confusion and ignorance.

'Well, I should wonder at that, gentlemen. Its arrival in this country has made every newspaper over the past few weeks.'

'Do not be too dismayed, Inspector — until recently Holmes and I have been travelling extensively abroad and we have barely had time to catch a breath since our return,' I explained and I observed a look of approval from Holmes at my refusal to grant the upper hand to the man from Scotland Yard.

Bradstreet was now clearly abashed and he wasted no time in detailing his problem to us.

'The facts then are these, gentlemen. Several weeks ago the museum in Bloomsbury acquired the rights to display a mandolin that is fashioned entirely out of solid gold. Its point of origin is unknown, although many historians believe that it was a gift to his wife from an emperor of ancient China. Its value is deemed to be incalculable and obviously it is quite irreplaceable.

'During the day, the display area has been heavily guarded and at the end of the day, once the last visitor has departed, the mandolin has been removed to a secure storeroom in the museum's basement. The room has no windows . . . '

'Obviously, there would be no need for them in a basement,' Holmes interrupted impatiently.

'Quite so, quite so. The door has been reinforced with iron girders and extra locks. The room is quite impenetrable and yet, this morning, when the guards returned to retrieve their charge, they found the room to be empty!'

'So you have turned to me to solve what is nothing more than a simple case of burglary?' Holmes asked incredulously.

'It is hardly a simple case, Mr Holmes, or I should not have bothered you at all.

It is inexplicable, I would say, for there are no signs at all of the door, nor the locks, having been interfered with and the walls and floor are solid and sound.' Bradstreet paused to see if Holmes' interest had yet been aroused. In that, he was to be sorely disappointed and Holmes suddenly returned to his work on the blackboard without a word or a glance to the desperate detective. Thereupon, Bradstreet decided to play his final and strongest card.

'I should also mention that the diplomatic pressure on me is enormous, for the mandolin has been loaned to the museum, for only a limited period, by none other than the Doge of Venice! The repercussions are potentially catastrophic and so I have come to you, Mr Holmes, as my last and only hope.'

Holmes was still facing the blackboard when Bradstreet had concluded his final plea, so the inspector collected his hat and began to make for the door, a crestfallen and anxious man.

'What of the ceiling?' Holmes asked, although his back was still turned to the centre of the room.

Bradstreet detected a glimmer of hope and he was smiling when he made his reply.

'As with the walls and floor, it has been constructed out of solid stone and there are no indications of interference.'

Bradstreet waited expectantly while Holmes went over to the fireplace to fill his old briar pipe with the contents of his Persian slipper.

'I suppose,' Holmes paused while he drew from his pipe, 'that there are certain elements of interest in your problem, Inspector Bradstreet.' Holmes encouraged the detective with a brief half smile and Bradstreet was clearly much relieved when he removed his hat once more. Holmes' vanity would never allow him to refuse the opportunity of being the 'last hope' and he invited the inspector to return to his seat with an extravagant sweep of his arm.

'What steps have been taken thus far, Inspector?'

'Obviously, a thorough search has been made of the strong room and this was subsequently extended to the ground floor of the museum itself. However, the search has revealed nothing so far, although I have ensured that the scene of the crime has remained undisturbed and ready for your inspection.'

Holmes nodded his appreciation.

'Are you satisfied that the mandolin had been secured the night before in the customary manner?'

'Oh absolutely, I have interviewed the guards who had been responsible for its safety over the past few days and they have confirmed independently that the mandolin had been placed securely inside when the strong room had been locked for the night. I must say that the museum has taken every possible precaution.

'The guards around the mandolin during the day are changed at regular intervals and the ones by night are rotated every couple of days. Furthermore, each guard possesses only one key, so that it is impossible to open the door unless both guards are present.'

'As you say, Inspector, the theft does

appear to have been an impossible task,' I commented.

'Yet it does seem to have taken place. Your little puzzle certainly has features of merit, Inspector,' Holmes murmured thoughtfully and there was a long pause while he drew from his pipe. 'Have your enquiries established the proven integrity of the guards?'

'As far as I can ascertain, they have all been employed by the museum for a number of years and they have retained unblemished records throughout that time. Of course, that does not rule out the possibility that two of the guards might have been working in tandem. So I have instructed my men to keep each pair under close surveillance until we are satisfied that their behaviour is in no way deemed to be suspicious.'

'It seems that you have left no stone unturned Inspector,' I observed.

I looked towards my friend who was lost in deep thought amid a plume of his aromatic tobacco. Although I gave no voice to my thoughts I began to wonder if it was no more than a coincidence that this important theft had occurred at the very location of our deadly final confrontation with the insidious Professor Ronald Sydney. Perhaps the dramatic events of that night and the adventures and revelations that had preceded them had left my mind too receptive to the notion of a further complex conspiracy?

I was wondering whether the same notion had occurred to my friend when Holmes suddenly broke through his reverie and turned towards a most perplexed Inspector Bradstreet.

'Inspector Bradstreet, I really fail to see what further contribution I can make towards your most thorough investigation. After all, you have already surveyed the scene of the crime and set in motion a series of investigations directed towards the only conceivable suspects! What more can I possibly add?'

'What you always add, Mr Holmes, your ability to see what others cannot and your talent for knowing what others do not. You could probably glance around that strong room and in an instant discover a clue that my men and I had overlooked after a day of careful examination!'

The sincerity of Bradstreet's entreaties clearly had a positive effect upon Holmes' previous indifference. He had been moved by Bradstreet's compliments and replaced his chalk upon the table. Then he picked up a sheet of paper and a pencil and hurriedly scribbled out a brief note.

'This note of mine will summon the only person in London who will already have more knowledge than you and I of the matter,' Holmes responded to the querying glances of both Bradstreet and me.

'You have sent for Menachem Goldman!' I exclaimed.

'Indeed I have, friend Watson. Mrs Hudson!'

A moment later our beleaguered landlady arrived breathlessly at our door and Holmes thrust the note into her outstretched hand.

'Would you be so good as to ensure that the butcher's boy receives this in the shortest time possible?' Holmes smiled.

'Do you ever send a note that is not extremely urgent?' she asked.

'Thank you Mrs Hudson.' Holmes almost closed the door on the poor woman's hand and we could hear her muttering to herself as she hurried down the stairs to do his bidding.

At this point I should explain that Menachem Goldman was Holmes' portal through to the seedier side of the jewellery trade. That is not to say that the man was actively involved in the illegal procurement of valuable items, but his vast knowledge and network of important contacts rendered him a profitable interest in their movements. He had been of immeasurable help during Holmes' investigation into the theft of Charlemagne's armour and he was a pivotal figure at the conclusion of an affair that I had entitled 'The Adventure of the Christmas Stocking'.

Many years ago he had adopted the street persona of an orthodox Polish rabbi. To this day I could not tell you if the guise was of tangible help during the course of Goldman's work, or whether it simply appealed to his sense of humour, but his impersonation was so thorough that he had even grown his sideburns so that they had become long and straggly! His strong Polish accent was flawless and he punctuated his speech with a liberal splattering of that unique, hybrid language known as Yiddish.[2] Once he had removed his beard and large-rimmed hat however, all traces of his public self would disappear and he even spoke with clipped, round London tones.

'Who, in heavens name, is this Menachem Goldman?' Bradstreet demanded to know.

Holmes appeared to be surprisingly embarrassed at this question and he hesitated before making his reply for what had seemed to be an age.

'Well, let us just say that Goldman has a unique and profound insight into the underbelly of the jewellery market, without ever having his character or reputation tarnished by his involvement in the odious and murky world that he inhabits and thrives in.'

'Well I am certainly relieved to hear

you say that, Mr Holmes,' Bradstreet sighed.

'You must not be too scrupulous when selecting your professional allies, Inspector, for the war against injustice throws together some strange bedfellows at times. Suffice it to say that Goldman's knowledge of the mandolin affair probably exceeds even yours, Inspector, and his involvement will likely save you hours of tedious work.'

'Well then, if you put it quite like that, Mr Holmes, I shall not be churlish enough to turn aside his help. Nevertheless, I would still be grateful if you could spare the time to run your eye over the museum's strong room.'

Holmes stared forlornly towards his blackboard before responding to Bradstreet's request.

'It seems that I shall need more data before I can get to the bottom of this matter, so I shall make every effort to attend the museum before it closes for the day. However, I beseech you to keep the room secure; otherwise my visit will prove to be a complete waste of time! In the mean time I must ask you both to leave me to my work.' Without another word or glance to either of us, Holmes wiped out his previous work and picked up his stick of chalk once again.

Bradstreet crept from the room somewhat bashfully and I found myself left to my own devices. I picked up my copy of General Lew Wallace's monumental tome *Ben-Hur: A Tale of the Christ* but found that its wordy descriptiveness could not hold my attention for more than twenty minutes. I took my pipe over to the window, being careful not to make a sound that might distract Holmes from his work, but soon found that the oppressiveness, created by Holmes' intensity, was becoming overwhelming. I found the confines of my bedroom to be too claustrophobic and so, without a word, I grabbed my hat and coat and decided to clear my head in the autumnal air outside.

I strode off at a brisk pace, but this soon slowed once I had realized that I had no destination in mind. It was inconceivable that, with two cases in progress, I should have found myself to be so singularly unemployed and once again my mind began to grapple with the notion that Holmes and I had become embroiled within the coils of an unfathomable conspiracy. Time and again the same names and locations seemed to bring themselves to our attention and for once, it seemed that Holmes was as unenlightened as I.

My friend seemed to attach more importance to the riddle presented to us by Denbigh Grey than I would have warranted, although the notion that Theodore Daxer might prove to be that elusive third member of the unholy trinity was one that I found to be irresistible. I shook my head repeatedly and lit a cigarette while I assessed the location to which my aimless walk had brought me.

For an inexplicable reason I had been compelled to travel southwards and I found myself halfway down Regents Street and moving towards Piccadilly. It soon became obvious to me that I was being drawn towards Charing Cross Road by my own instincts and before too long I found myself staring up at the magnificent façade of the Garrick Theatre. I was amazed that I had completed that two-mile trek in less than thirty minutes and my pulse quickened as I gazed up at the billboard. There, halfway down the list of characters and players and alongside the description of her character, Lady Macduff, was the name that I had sought from the outset: Sophie Sinclair.

I had arrived with time enough to spare before the matinee performance of Shakespeare's *Macbeth*, so I spent a while in admiring the building's magnificent architecture, which was very much in the style of the late Italian Renaissance. There was a long balcony, covered by an elaborate arcade and I discovered that the interior was similarly ornate, being decorated with mosaics, parquetry and an unusual abundance of colossal mirrors.

I realized, with some surprise, that despite the fact that the Garrick had been open for over seven years, this was to be my first visit there and I wasted no time in securing my ticket for the fourth row of the front stalls, arguably the best and most expensive in the house. The auditorium was surprisingly large and boasted a selection of boxes together with both a broad lower and upper circle.

However, I decided that the intimacy of the stalls was more suitable for my purposes and I consequently shrugged off the extra cost. I made my way up to the arcade, with a glass of whiskey and a final cigarette, before readying myself for the performance of the 'Scottish Play', as superstitious thespians preferred to name it. Naturally enough, I was disappointed to note that the role of Lady Macduff was afforded very little stage time, but I was certain that the long wait for her appearance would be worth it.

4

The Scottish Play

As the curtain slowly rose, I became enwrapped by that familiar feeling of anticipation and excitement, although on this occasion my true reason for being present heightened that effect somewhat.

I thoroughly enjoyed the first act. It was well produced and performed and I thrilled at the delivery of all of those familiar lines. From the opening with the three crones, the death of King Duncan and the angst of Lady Macbeth, each one brought me back to a bleak, unearthly view of medieval Scotland. I could almost feel the chill of the harsh, heathland winds and the roll of the dark, ominous mists.

By the time that the intermission arrived, my anticipation at the thought of seeing Miss Sinclair again compelled me to return to the arcade with a second drink. Furthermore, when she did finally make her long-awaited entrance, it was all that I could do to refrain from giving her a rousing standing ovation, before she had even uttered a single line! From my privileged vantage point I was able to recall my reasons for being there and even her costume and make-up did nothing to obscure the natural physical advantages with which she was so fortuitously endowed.

Sadly, her presence on the stage was to be as short lived as one would have expected and she and her 'little chickens' were soon to be surrounded and ruthlessly slaughtered by Macbeth's assassins! The scene was as dramatic and as heartfelt as I had always remembered it to be, but I soon realized that there was an unusual deviation from the original text, for reasons that I could not yet fathom. The assassins stood over their pathetic victims for far longer than was usual and a terrible, unscripted on-stage shriek of horror echoed around the entire auditorium.

The entire scene became drowned in

noise and confusion as the back stage staff began to shepherd the shell-shocked cast from the stage and into the wings. Slowly the players deserted the stage and all that remained, before too long, were the stage-hands and the prostrate form of Sophie Sinclair. An unusually large pool of blood was seeping out from under her body and I soon realized that it was not artificial.

Without a moment's thought or delay, I leapt up onto the stage and attempted to assume temporary control of the situation. The stage manager requested that the audience should exit the building in a calm and orderly fashion, while I asked the stagehands to ensure that every member of the cast remain backstage until they had been questioned by the police.

However, my immediate concern was to ascertain the full extent of Miss Sinclair's injuries and to contain them prior to the arrival of the police. I could see at once that a single deep puncture, caused by a small but lethal dagger, had penetrated her with some force. Fortunately, the would-be killer had missed his mark, for the wound was over an inch below her heart and she still breathed.

I could tell, from the crimson pool that surrounded her, that she had lost a considerable amount of blood already and that this could not continue unabated for too much longer without her life ebbing away. Fortunately her character was wearing a small white apron over her costume and I quickly tore this from her before folding it into a makeshift surgical pad. Once this was in place, I called for a cloak that had been worn by one of the guards and I tore this into thick equal strips, which I wrapped firmly around her body to aid the pad in stemming the flow of blood.

Once I was satisfied that this had been successful, I called for a cushion and managed to roll her onto her side to help divert the blood away from her lungs. There was clearly nothing more that I could do under those circumstances and once I was satisfied that she was relatively comfortable, I ensured that Lady Macduff's assassins were segregated from the rest of the cast and ready for questioning.

To my great relief, it was at this moment that the police arrived with stretcher bearers in close attendance and I watched apprehensively as they carried Miss Sinclair carefully away to an ambulance. My immediate instinct was to go with them, but I soon realized that any leader of the investigation would surely insist on interviewing me there and then. I just had time to establish that they were taking her to Saint Thomas' Hospital, on Westminster Bridge Road, when a familiar figure appeared upon the stage.

'Well, upon my word it's none other than Dr Watson! What in heaven's name are you doing here? Surely it is not yet another strange coincidence?'

I was as taken aback as he, for I found myself face to face with our old friend Inspector Lestrade. His gaunt face was as contorted with as much anxiety and confusion as was usual for him, perhaps a little more so on this occasion.

'I can assure you, Inspector, that there is no coincidence in my being here at all.'

As he pulled out his notebook I outlined the exact circumstances that had led me to the Garrick Theatre that day and I detailed every measure that I had taken since the tragedy had occurred on stage. He congratulated me upon my quick thinking and rapid response and immediately reassured me that he would inform me of Miss Sinclair's condition as soon as he received that information from the hospital. In the meantime, however, he requested that I remain to aid him in his investigations.

I acquiesced at once, but I was aghast once I realized that Lestrade had arrived with only three constables in attendance. After all, the theatre was a vast building that had been endowed with a labyrinthine network of tunnels and corridors, dressing rooms and store-rooms, each one of which was capable of concealing a resourceful fugitive. I immediately informed Lestrade that I had arranged for the segregation of the assassins from the remainder of the cast, a course of action that pleased him at first.

Lestrade despatched his constables to ensure that nobody should pass through any of the rear exits, while he was waiting to be led through to the largest of the dressing rooms so that he could begin the process of interviewing the assassins, each one in turn. I volunteered to instigate a search for the murder weapon.

'You are certain that the wounds of Miss Sinclair were not caused accidentally?' Lestrade asked before beginning his investigation. 'After all, there was a great deal of confusion during the attack upon her character and as far as I understand it, a good many weapons were employed during the assault. Surely such a notion is not unfeasible?'

I did not give Lestrade's suggestion even a moment's credence and I shook my head emphatically.

'If you were to examine the wound closely, you would also be in little doubt that the depth of the wound and the force required to make such an insertion could only have been the result of a deliberate assault. Besides, a great deal of care is taken to ensure that the stage props are quite blunt. No, Inspector, we are surely investigating a case of wilful attempted murder!'

'It is hard to believe that anybody would wish to do away with a harmless, aspiring young actress such as Sophie Sinclair. What could possibly have been the motive for such a crime, I wonder?' Lestrade asked thoughtfully.

'Ah well,' I hesitated for several moments before making my reply. 'Any notion that we might formulate can only be purely speculative at this early stage. However, we should not forget that Miss Sinclair had been deeply involved with John Vincent Harden for some time and as we both know he lied repeatedly about having been a member of the Diogenes Club. The integrity of that singular establishment has been brought into question on many occasions in recent weeks and its secrets are many.

'Inspector, you know as well as I how ruthlessly the powers behind recent events have covered their tracks. Any secrets that Harden might have passed on, even inadvertently, to Miss Sinclair would have died with her had the assailant not missed his mark. If I were you, Inspector Lestrade, I should waste no time in despatching an officer to watch over her, on a twenty-four hour vigil.'

Lestrade's gaunt features turned quite ashen once he had given my words due consideration and it was only when he had issued instructions to his men that he set about interviewing the assassins. At least he had displayed the good sense to call for reinforcements from Scotland Yard and as soon as they had arrived we began the thankless task of searching for the knife.

While I had awaited the arrival of the extra constables, I thumbed my way idly through an abandoned programme. Apart from that of Miss Sinclair, I also recognized the names of several of the leading players from previous productions, but unfortunately the names of the assassins had not been individualized. I tossed the redundant brochure back onto the seat and smoked a cigarette before beginning the search.

The constables and I were meticulous

in our survey of each and every nook and cranny, with which the theatre was so plentifully endowed. It was only once we had concluded our unproductive search that I realized with astonishment and dismay that Lestrade had dismissed every member of the cast who had not been allocated the role of an assassin. To an experienced performer, a quick change of costume would be a relatively easy act to carry out and as a consequence there was no guarantee that the assailant was even still in the building.

I pointed this fact out to Lestrade, once he had concluded the last of his fruitless interviews. He stared vacantly ahead for several moments until the significance of my appraisal finally registered with him. Once again, he shook his head forlornly and rather uncharitably vented his anger and frustration upon his hapless subordinates.

'Did your interviews shed any light upon the debacle on stage?' I asked, although in all honesty, I did not expect a reply that was any different to the one that I received.

'I cannot believe that of the seven actors that I have spoken to, not even one had been aware of or noticed anything unusual or untoward taking place,' Lestrade complained bitterly.

'Perhaps they were used to a scene of commotion every time that the attack was performed? The assault upon Miss Sinclair was undoubtedly a well-conceived crime, for the nature of the scene itself formed a perfect piece of camouflage,' I offered speculatively.

'As you say Dr Watson, a most well-conceived plan indeed!' Lestrade lamented.

Then a thought occurred to me and with a rush of excitement I hurried back to the seat on which I had deposited the discarded programme. Sure enough, my memory had not deceived me and I hastened back to Lestrade to show him my findings.

'Inspector Lestrade, are you absolutely certain that you only interviewed seven assassins?' I asked breathlessly, knowing too well the inevitable reply that I would receive. Lestrade seemed to be somewhat put out when he reluctantly pulled out his notebook once again.

'Dr Watson, you know only too well how meticulous I am with my investigations. See here, I have listed each name and an accurate report of every reply. As you can see, there are only seven names!'

'I apologize for having doubted you Inspector, but this programme numbers them as eight. One has surely slipped through your net and I'll wager he is the man we are looking for! I take it that every exit has been manned by one your constables?'

Lestrade nodded emphatically.

'In that case Miss Sinclair's assailant must still be in the building. Although by now I am certain that he is no longer in the guise of one of Lady Macduff's executioners. We must instigate a search at once.'

Lestrade agreed without hesitation and a moment later I found myself in the wing adjacent to the stage that housed the various dressing rooms and prop stores. I had been allocated the corridor that led out to the rear exit on St Martin's Lane.

The passageway was long, dark and ominously silent and my footsteps created a resonant echo. Although the majority of the Garrick had been illuminated by electricity, at that time the peripheral sections were still being lit by gas. The lamps were few and sparse and soon the shadows that they created were causing me to regret the absence of both my army revolver and my friend, Sherlock Holmes.

I slowed my pace and softened my steps, for I did not want my approach to be so obvious. Nevertheless, I soon found myself at the St Martin's Lane exit, without having seen nor heard anything untoward. The constable on duty there seemed sensible and vigilant and he assured me that not a soul had passed his way, neither dressed as an assassin nor otherwise. I explained to him the necessity for an increase in his diligence and then I slowly retraced my steps.

I had barely gone a few yards when I heard a faint scuff upon the stone floor behind me. I immediately dismissed it as nothing more than my imagination or perhaps an echo of my own cautious steps.

However, by the time that I had heard the second scrape and accorded it more significance, it was too late! I caught a flash of blue from the constable's uniform and a long, threatening object in his fast-moving hand. The crown of my head erupted in shattering pain and I felt myself falling towards the floor, unable to support myself. The pain caused by a searing white light forced me to close my eyes and the last sound that I heard, before oblivion engulfed me, was that of the 'constable' sprinting towards the unguarded exit.

When consciousness finally returned to me I discovered that the pain to my head had not diminished. My first instinct was to close my eyes once more and hope that further sleep might aid my recovery. However, I then realized that my circumstances had altered somewhat, for I was no longer on the stone floor within the Garrick Theatre, but safely within my own bed back in Baker Street.

As my vision slowly improved, I

recognized Mrs Hudson hovering awkwardly by my bedside and she was clutching a promising looking tray of refreshments. I also recognized my old friend standing beside her and at that moment I wondered whether the blow to my head had brought on a state of delirium. For Sherlock Holmes was smiling down upon me with a look of concern on his face such as I had rarely seen before and he was holding a damp flannel with which he had been daubing my throbbing head.

'My dear fellow, you really must try to curtail that careless and reckless side of your nature. After all there is much work to be done and my effectiveness is much diminished without my Doctor by my side!'

Holmes' features remained as inscrutable as ever, so that I did not know whether I should be laughing or apologizing. Holmes immediately recognized my confusion, however, and assured me of his jest by insisting that I return to my rest once I had partaken of Mrs Hudson's offerings. I followed both of his instructions with enthusiasm and did not awake again until the following morning.

It was only then that I felt strong enough to leave my bed and I joined Holmes at the breakfast table for a cup of coffee and a review of our current situation. Holmes stared at me for an age, before he was satisfied that my improved condition would allow me to take a practical interest in our endless list of cases.

'As invaluable as your opinion is to me, I would not consider burdening you unless I was certain that your health had considerably progressed.' Despite his concern for me, there was an optimistic expectation in his voice that I could not ignore. My injury was now nothing more than a dull headache and I smiled at Holmes with an emphatic reassurance.

'As ever, Holmes, I am here to be used, although I would first like to learn of how my return to Baker Street came about and the sequel to the events at the Garrick.'

'Oh Watson, it is a relief to have you

back in harness, I must say!' I was pleased to observe that Holmes' declaration was a genuine expression of the value that he attached to my support.

Holmes lit a cigarette and moved over to the window. It was only then that I realized how a deep, ominous fog had descended upon Baker Street and that, coupled to an added intensity in Holmes' tone, provoked an involuntary shiver in me as I sensed that our investigations had reached a portentous crossroads.

'You will be glad to hear that once the gravity of your injuries had been assessed and you had been returned safely to Baker Street, I engaged Lestrade in a lengthy consultation. As far as I can ascertain, you did remarkably well, Watson, and I am certain that matters would have reached a far sorrier pass had it not been for your intervention. I will not dwell upon your dubious motives for having visited the theatre in the first place, but notwithstanding them, your presence was indeed most timely and fortuitous.

'You may console yourself with the

knowledge that your adversary at the rear exit was not acting alone and that the attempt upon Miss Sinclair's life was part of a cleverly conceived scheme, devised by an individual with a far broader canvas!'

'No doubt you are referring to the third and as yet unidentified member of the unholy trinity!' I declared.

More often than not, Holmes would have chastised me for having made so bold and unsubstantiated an assumption. On this occasion and to my great relief, that was not to be the case.

'Very likely, yes,' he replied with a disconcerting and hushed air of concern. Holmes appeared to be so troubled, in fact, that he found it almost impossible to look at me while he continued with his analysis of the current situation.

'You should know, Watson, that my interview with Lestrade and my subsequent inquiries at the museum have confirmed that there is a solid foundation beneath your hypothesis. Although we are no closer to identifying and apprehending Miss Sinclair's assailant, Lestrade has informed me that by further questioning the play's assassins he has established a clear description of your counterfeit constable. I need not burden you with the details; however I can confirm that this individual has been extraordinarily industrious!

'Despite the close attentions of Bradstreet's best men, we have now established that one of the museum's night guards has somehow slipped through their fingers. The man in question had been the museum's most recent recruitment, yet more tellingly his employment had been confirmed by none other than the late Professor Sydney, of notorious repute.'

'Good heavens Holmes, that man's influence extends even from beyond the grave!' I exclaimed.

'Indeed it does Watson and his dying threats and warnings certainly carry more credence than I would have ascribed to them. However, I will warrant that even your vivid imagination would not dwell too long upon the notion that the missing guard's description would correspond exactly with that of the Garrick's resourceful assassin.' Holmes hushed my next expletive by raising a defensive hand.

'However Doctor, all is not yet lost, I assure you. Although my examination of the museum's strong room was as fruitless as that of Bradstreet and his merry band, I was able to justify Bradstreet's coercion with a small discovery that I made at the very point of my departure. As you have already heard, it is impossible for one man alone to open the strong room door, indeed even two would find it hard to pull this weighty monolith into position.

'Obviously the notion that the thief had managed to procure a second key had already occurred to me, but my discovery of a small pile of cigarette ash just outside the door is a clear indication that there had been a small delay to the execution of this enterprise. Who, in their right mind, would pause for a smoke, at the very point of carrying out such a perilous undertaking, unless they were waiting for the arrival of another?'

'There must have been an accomplice,

of course!' I confirmed excitedly.

'My thoughts exactly, friend Watson and unless I am very much mistaken the very man that can aid us in identifying this mysterious accomplice has just arrived at our door.'

I had been so engrossed with Holmes' startling revelations that I had not even been aware of the sound of the doorbell being pulled. A moment later, Mrs Hudson showed Menachem Goldman to our room.

It was always a pleasure to meet with one of Holmes' more occasional accomplices. His street disguise, which I have described earlier, did nothing to diminish his broad, beaming smile and the warm, mischievous glint in his eyes. He shook our hands vigorously and then rubbed his own together in anticipation of a new and intriguing challenge from Holmes. Of course if there proved to be a small profit to be had at the conclusion, then he would not be averse to that either!

Despite the time of year, Goldman appeared relieved to be able to remove his long black coat and hat, which he did without a moment's hesitation.

'What a schlep, Mr Holmes!' Goldman exclaimed while removing copious amounts of perspiration from his brow with a grubby silk handkerchief.

Holmes understood Goldman's meaning and immediately waved him to a chair. He poured him a substantial whiskey from the decanter.

'Perhaps this will go some way towards revitalizing you?' Holmes suggested with a smile.

'Oh yes indeed, Mr Holmes, you are a proper *mensch*!'

'As culturally enriching to hear as it undoubtedly is, I think you can safely dispense with the Yiddish, whilst in our company, Mr Goldman.'

'Oh Mr Holmes, but I do need to keep it up you know!' Goldman laughed, although he was now as far removed from an orthodox Polish Jew as one could imagine. 'I sense that you are now about to get down to business.'

Holmes confirmed this statement with a sharp nod of his head and he lit his old briar pipe.

'What do you know of the object known as the Venetian mandolin?' Holmes asked.

'The question should have been what don't I know about the Venetian mandolin!' Goldman's eyes sparkled once again.

'I do already possess a limited knowledge of its history, although that is now rather irrelevant to me. My immediate concern is with its current whereabouts and fate,' Holmes replied.

'Ah, so you are trying to find out if I am aware of its theft from the museum, are you not? Well I would say that it is fairly obvious that I do . . . '

'How is that possible?' I interrupted. 'The story has not even been released to the newspapers yet.'

Goldman pressed his forefinger to his temple.

'Dr Watson, my special insights into affairs of this nature is the reason for Mr Holmes summoning me here today, is it not?' Goldman switched his attention to Holmes for confirmation. Holmes merely smiled his substantiation.

'Do not trouble yourself, Menachem, I

will not pry into the source of your knowledge, nor is it necessary that I do so. I merely wish to know where the mandolin currently resides.'

'You say merely, Mr Holmes, but I assure you that which you ask for is a piece of information that is not so easy to come by. Furthermore, should I be able to aid you in its recovery, there is very little chance that a reward will be forthcoming from so anonymous a source.' Goldman smiled mischievously while holding out his hand.

'Your subtle approach is not lost on me and I assure you that you will be suitably compensated should the matter be successfully concluded,' Holmes confirmed resignedly.

'Mr Holmes, I fear that I might be treading into treacherous territory on your behalf and a small compensation on the outset might provide me with a greater incentive.' Goldman smiled and his hand remained outstretched towards Holmes.

With a feigned reluctance, Holmes reached into his pocket and then folded a paper incentive into Goldman's eager palm.

'Mind you, Mr Goldman, I shall expect results within forty-eight hours!' Holmes declared.

Goldman merely shrugged his shoulders and began to reassemble his Polish guise while he made his way towards the door.

'*Oy vey!*' he exclaimed in his best Yiddish. 'Do not be too surprised if I return with news within twenty-four hours.' With a confident jaunt, Menachem Goldman took his leave.

5

The Death of Langdale Pike

'Well, you certainly cannot accuse that man of lacking in confidence,' I declared jovially while closing the door behind Goldman.

'I assure you, Watson, that the faith that he has in his own ability is not without foundation. Do not mistake his eccentricities for stupidity and arrogance.'

At this point, Holmes picked up his chalk once more and he was about to return to his work upon the blackboard, when I decided to intercede and finally voice the misgivings that I had been harbouring for some time.

'Holmes,' I began tentatively. 'Although I fully understand the importance that you attach to the code of Denbigh Grey, I cannot for the life of me understand your reluctance to discuss the potential significance of our other recent cases. After all, each one of them is connected in some way to either the Diogenes Club or the Bloomsbury Museum and we both well remember the dark paths that those venerable establishments have previously led us upon.'

Holmes responded with an impatient grunt and a look of resigned irritation. He replaced his chalk with reluctance and returned to his chair with a lighted pipe.

'Carry on.' He glared impatiently.

I must confess to having been somewhat intimidated by Holmes' aggressive entreaty and I swallowed deeply and repeatedly before continuing with my supposition. Holmes' half smile showed me that my discomfiture had not been lost on him.

'Had the death of John Vincent Harden and the extraordinary circumstances that surrounded it been an isolated incident, I would probably have put it down to nothing more than mere coincidence. However the attack upon his former paramour shortly afterward and the fact that Sophie Sinclair's assailant was none other than the perpetrator of the theft of the Venetian mandolin certainly indicates that a single force might be behind all three crimes.

'Furthermore, when you consider the fact that this individual had been employed by the very man that we helped destroy and then the scale of the insidious organization that had surrounded him — well then I fail to understand your refusal to at least voice some misgivings. Even if these crimes were not directly connected, I would have expected you to consider the possibility that they have been presented to us as a means of a diversion from our quest to identify the elusive third member of the unholy trinity!' By the conclusion of my address I had raised my voice considerably, due to my frustration at Holmes' detached reaction to my every word.

Holmes raised his eyebrow quizzically and he appeared to be rather disappointed at my loss of temper. He shook his head dejectedly.

'Oh Watson, of course these notions of yours have also occurred to me, but I have chosen not to dwell upon such speculation until such time as I have assembled some tangible evidence that might substantiate them. You have also chosen not to mention the fact that the case of the Egyptian gargoyle is patently disconnected from the others.

'I have chosen, therefore, to devote my time to the more significant task of breaking down a code that has been fed mysteriously to one of the most dangerous men in Europe.' This time it was Holmes' turn to raise his voice in frustration.

Holmes could see that his somewhat hostile rebuttal had left me rather crestfallen and consequently his next remark to me was in a softer tone. He was aimlessly toying with his chalk before his frustration caused him to snap it deliberately upon the board.

'Despite my best endeavours, however, I am now almost resigned to the fact that I shall be unable to make further progress until I receive additional data from Denbigh Grey. In the meantime I shall give your notions their due attention,' Holmes conceded.

'Thank you, Holmes.'

For now, Holmes seemed to be ready to accept defeat and he was on the point of assuming the lotus position on his armchair when I broached the subject of his brother Mycroft's potential involvement with the activities of the trinity.

Holmes laughed off my suggestion with a dismissive disdain and it was several minutes before he was able to formulate an articulate response.

'I take it that your theory is based upon the fact that Mycroft is a prominent member of a club whose motives have recently come under some close scrutiny?' Holmes asked and he was still barely able to suppress his amusement.

'Oh come along, Holmes!' I protested. 'Even I would hardly be likely to voice such a proposal based merely on that single fact.'

I went on to explain that I had seen the symbol of an owl at the base of a wire he had received and discarded into a cold fire, from a contact of his from Bavaria, which had answered his inquiries into the Bavarian Brotherhood. At the time, I had found the presence of a painting of an owl on the wall of Mycroft's office to be most suggestive.

'Surely you must have been surprised at the manner in which Mycroft had followed our progress through Italy and Egypt?' I continued. 'He seemed to have been dogging our every step and he was so certain of the time of our arrival in London that he had even arranged for Gunner King to be waiting for us at the station with his cab!'

I had been so certain of my ground that I had concluded my summation in a most emphatic fashion. However, Holmes had not been moved either by my words or by the manner of their delivery. He even responded in the same amused manner that he previously found so hard to suppress.

'Really Watson, as admirable as a vivid imagination can often be, sometimes it is necessary to rein it in and bring it under control. Otherwise, as in this instance, it will lead you upon a most merry dance. Have I not told you, on more than one occasion, that my brother is to all intents and purposes the central exchange of information for the entire British government?'

I nodded my confirmation.

'Do you think it likely then that a man in such an illustrious and imperative position would place under threat the very edifice that he has devoted so many years of sterling service to? Of course not, for that would negate all that he has achieved and believed in. He has been horrified by the flagrant manner in which his club has been abused and he will do anything in his power to restore it to its former standing.

'He was able to keep track of our comings and goings because the long arm of his influence enabled him to do so and because he wanted to, purely out of concern for our safety and wellbeing. His close surveillance of us posed no threat whatsoever and King's presence at the station was a further demonstration of Mycroft's bounty. As for the owl . . . well perhaps he just happens to like owls eh?'

'You are right, of course,' I mumbled, now feeling totally embarrassed by the admission of my own foolishness.

'Do not chastise yourself too heavily, my friend, for at least we can now be certain that we have eliminated the impossible and we can progress to a more logical conclusion.'

With that, Holmes picked up a piece of the chalk that he had just broken so petulantly and turned towards the black-board once more.

'What progress have you made so far with the deciphering?' I asked quietly and tentatively.

'None at all, I am afraid to say.' Holmes turned towards me and I could see that his frustration was now manoeuvring him towards one of his brown moods.

For a moment I had feared that his despondence would turn his attention towards his Moroccan leather case and the implements of his darkest dependency that it contained. Thankfully my worst fears were not to be realized and he sank dejectedly into his chair by the fire with a lighted cigarette.

'I am concerned, Watson, for I was certain that we would have heard from

Grey by now. Why does he not come?' he asked and there was an unanswerable appeal in his bloodshot eyes that I could not respond to. All I could offer to him was a heavy shrug of my shoulders and I had a similar question of my own, regarding Mrs Hudson and our lunch!

My question was answered a few moments later, when our landlady appeared bearing a tray of bread, cheese and coffee. I tore into these with a ravenous urgency and entreated my friend to join me. When I turned around, however, I could see that the cigarette had been abandoned and he was now in a state of deep meditation with his eyes tightly closed.

I knew from my previous experience that any attempt by me at communication would be futile and I allowed Mrs Hudson to remove his empty plate with resignation. I decided to make a further attempt at digesting Ben-Hur and discovered, to my relief and surprise, that it did in fact improve as it progressed. Nevertheless, before too long I fell into a deep sleep, no doubt lulled by the glow from the fire and a small port that I had followed my lunch with. I was only disturbed from my slumber when a large burnt cinder from the dying fire fell down upon the grate.

Lunch seemed to meld into supper and then into an evening tray of tea, yet still my friend remained in the lotus position and any revelations that might have been occurring to him for now remained an enigma. Once I was certain that there was little likelihood of Holmes abandoning his contemplations at a reasonable hour, I decided to retire for the night, disappointed that I had received no further insight into the progress of our case.

As a consequence, it proved to be a restless night, and my mind was constantly regurgitating the multitude of questions that still remained unanswered. Therefore, I was well able to respond sharply to the commotion at our door, which had occurred at a little after six o'clock the following morning. I grabbed my army revolver, pulled on my gown and tore down the stairs in answer to Mrs Hudson's plaintive call.

To my great surprise, I found that Holmes had already answered our landlady's appeal and that he was in deep conversation with a young constable from Scotland Yard. Holmes' freshness and alertness belied his night-long sleepless vigil and he gracefully bounded up the stairs while calling for the constable and I to follow him.

By the time that the constable and I had joined him, Holmes was already in his chair and although he was sitting crossed legged, he was now in a more conventional position. He smoothed back his dishevelled hair and smiled encouragingly at the agitated young officer, while lighting his first cigarette of the day.

'Now Constable, I fervently suggest that you draw a deep breath before explaining to me the exact circumstances that have led you to my door at this unearthly hour.'

The nervous young fellow belatedly and apologetically removed his helmet and then cleared his throat, several times, before responding to Holmes' request.

'Sorry Mr 'olmes, for my unruly

arrival, but Inspector Gregson insisted that I bring you this news urgently.' The constable was clearly London born and bred and he was obviously excited at the prospect of being entrusted with such a burning and important mission.

'No need for apologies, Constable, the good inspector is often prone to excitability.' Holmes smiled.

'Well, the facts are these, Mr 'olmes. An associate of yours, who goes by the name of Langdale Pike, has been found murdered upon the floor of his private room, in his club on St James' Street. His time of death has not been fixed yet, because he was only discovered earlier this morning by the cleaning lady and he not been seen since the porter brought his supper and several glasses of cognac, the night before.' The constable seemed proud of his brief but coherent statement.

'Inspector Gregson is certain that this was a case of murder, even at such an early stage?' Holmes asked.

'Oh yes sir, although there was really no other conclusion that he could possibly have come to. You see, Pike's

146

throat had been cut open from ear to ear.'

Holmes and I immediately exchanged looks of alarm upon hearing of this most singular and savage form of attack and our minds immediately went back to the murderous events in Rome and Egypt. The effect that the words of this young constable had upon Holmes was both startling and profound. He emitted a low whistle and sank back into his chair in a manner that suggested that he too had suffered a sudden and violent assault. His face became ashen and taut and his brow tightened into a deep knot.

To my great surprise, he refused to question the constable further and he dismissed him with a silent and laboured flick of his hand. The young man seemed to be as bemused as I had been, but he took his leave nevertheless.

Holmes sat in a stone-faced silence for what had seemed to be an age. Although I was bursting with a mixture of excitement and horror, one look at my friend's grey countenance convinced me that now would not be the time to air my thoughts. Even if I had done so, I was certain that the same thoughts had also crossed Holmes' mind and I sat opposite to him in silent anticipation.

He growled silently to himself while lighting a cigarette with a violent stroke of his vesta.

'I have been guilty of a grave oversight, Watson, and I owe you a most humble apology for having been so dismissive of your succinct prognosis a while earlier.' He could not quite bring himself to look at me directly, so sincere was his sense of guilt, but I knew that the manner of Pike's murder had radically altered his view of the case.

I should now explain the nature of Holmes' association with Mr Langdale Pike. I could never pretend to Holmes that I approved of their special arrangement and I constantly recoiled at the thought of Pike's occupation. Pike had been a gossip columnist of the most disreputable type and he had always plied his nefarious trade within the corridors of power and privilege.

Notwithstanding the distress that Pike's column wrought amongst his victims and their families, Holmes often found himself calling upon Pike's services whenever he needed a portal into a world that would not normally have granted him access. However, Pike's guidance did come at a price and I was appalled at the indifference that Holmes often displayed on those occasions when he supplied Pike with material for his column.

Holmes would then turn away from my qualms and protestations and justify his immoral cooperation by pointing out the advantages that Pike supplied him with in his fight against crime and injustice. Holmes satisfied his conscience, or rather lack of it, with the age-old phrase that the ends justify the means, but it was an attitude that I found hard to reconcile to my own code of morals.

Nevertheless, I was convinced that Holmes' display of surprise and despondency upon hearing of Langdale Pike's death was born more from the manner of the death and its implications than any sense of loss or remorse. In any event, it came as no surprise to me to hear of Pike's untimely death, for the man surely had accumulated many vengeful enemies over the years.

'I had become so obsessed with the idea of breaking the code of Denbigh Grey, that I had lost sight of the fact that it might conceivably be connected with the other cases that have been thrust upon us of late with such alarming regularity,' Holmes continued.

'You mean that a clue to the code might be found within the details of our other investigations?' I asked.

'My thoughts exactly, Doctor! With that in mind, I will now despatch two urgent important invitations before we depart for St James' Street. Mrs Hudson!' he cried and an instant after he had completed his scrawled messages, we found ourselves upon Baker Street once more and in urgent need of a cab.

The hour was still early and therefore we had been able to avoid the traffic that would undoubtedly have accumulated within a short while. Holmes refused to be drawn upon the names of the recipients of his invitations, but assured me that I would discover their identities soon enough. He seemed to be determined to focus only upon the examination of Pike's room for now and at the exclusion of all else.

We pulled up outside a large, square Georgian building, which boasted a long flight of wide stone steps leading up to an enormous and ornate black door. Once we had passed through the front arch and the Ionian pillars, I stood in awe and gaped at the fabulous collection of artwork that adorned each wall of the atrium. However, I had very little time in which to admire them, for my friend had already tossed his hat and coat to a young footman and he was soon bounding silently up the richly carpeted stairs.

Holmes had evidently visited Pike on many less fraught occasions, for he found his way to Pike's private room without a moment's hesitation. We were met at the door by a brace of conscientious young constables, who had steadfastly refused us entry until the officer who had brought us the news to Baker Street confirmed our identity to them. Although anxious and impatient to gain immediate entry,

Holmes was equally impressed by their diligence.

He was pleased to hear that, on Gregson's instructions, nothing apart from Pike's body had been moved or touched, prior to our arrival. Holmes rubbed his hands together in anticipation of a broad and blank canvas upon which to ply his art and you would not have known, from his demeanour, that he was investigating the death of someone that he had known and worked with over a period of many years.

We followed Holmes into the large, airy room, although he begged us to move no further until he had completed his work. It was always an intriguing pleasure for me to observe Holmes as he set about extracting as much information as he could from an empty room. Each and every discovery that he made would invariably be invisible to any mortal man!

Upon hearing that the windows had been found closed and locked, Holmes began his work there. He slipped out his small magnifying glass and examined each surround and sill with a meticulous diligence. However, an impatient grunt indicated that his search had borne little fruit.

He turned his attention therefore to the carpeted floor and drew hurried circles around two small patches, without offering an explanation for either of them. He confirmed their importance, however, by measuring each one in turn with a small tape that he always had upon his person.

A large bloodstain indicated the position where Pike had fallen and upon seeing the area that it covered, I was left in little doubt that the attack had been a savage and brutal one.

Holmes was about to examine the table that still contained Pike's dinner tray and a small cluster of papers, when he turned towards the constables with a startling change of mind.

'Who actually raised the alarm and by what method?' Holmes asked with some urgency. The constables appeared to have been taken aback by Holmes' abruptness, but the one who seemed to be the older of the two eventually replied.

'The morning cleaner was the first

person to realize that something was amiss, when she failed to gain access to the room. She then called upon Mr Gabriel, the head porter, to investigate by using his pass key. As you can imagine, they were both shaken to the core by the sight of Mr Pike bleeding upon the floor and they soon despatched a messenger to Scotland Yard.'

'Yet the dinner tray was obviously delivered the night before. Did nobody seem surprised that Pike's dinner tray had not already been removed?' Holmes asked, although now his tone was somewhat calmer and more thoughtful.

'I am sure that the cleaner and Mr Gabriel gave it no thought at all ... under the circumstances I mean.' The same constable now stuttered his reply, as he was clearly affected by Holmes' intense glare.

'So it seems that Gabriel was not the porter who brought Pike his food last night. Have you managed to identify the porter who actually did so? After all, he was the last person to have seen Pike alive.'

'Yes sir, that would have been Dave Bowman, a young footman who Gabriel had only recently taken under his wing.'

'I should very much like to interview that young man, before I continue with my examination.' Holmes raised a suspicious eyebrow, as the young officer reddened and began to stumble over his words once more.

'I am sorry but that will not be possible, Mr Holmes,' he blurted out.

'Why is that and what has become of him, pray tell?' Holmes was now clearly agitated by what he construed as grave incompetence.

'I am afraid he is nowhere to be found,' the constable replied apologetically.

'I see. Did Inspector Gregson not find that to be in the least bit suspicious?' The constable's shrug spoke volumes and Holmes began to grind his teeth in frustration. 'Yet your inspector chose fit to desert the scene of the crime before he had ascertained the whereabouts of a key witness?'

The constable seemed to be embarrassed by Gregson's negligence; however

Holmes tried to ease the young man's discomfort with a warm smile and a timely suggestion.

'Well Constable, perhaps we can yet retrieve the situation? I would very much like you to obtain from Mr Gabriel a full description of the missing footman and the size of the uniform that he had been issued with. I am most particularly interested in the size of his boots.'

'I will see to it right away, Mr Holmes.' The constable turned sharply on his heels and he was off to do Holmes' bidding without a moment's hesitation, despite being surprised at the nature of his request.

During the constable's absence Holmes continued with his exploration for clues. He gingerly fingered the various items upon Pike's dinner tray and examined the table with infinite care. However, it was only when he picked up Pike's notebook for closer inspection that Holmes' manner suddenly altered and I recognized at once the look of exaltation that I had seen so often at the moment of success. He turned around and faced the remaining constable.

'I would suggest that you and your colleague immediately instigate a search for Dave Bowman,' Holmes suggested with authority. The constable hesitated before replying.

'I am sorry sir, but the inspector ordered us to remain in attendance at all times.'

'As admirable as your diligence surely is, you can be in no doubt that Mr Sherlock Holmes would never interfere with nor disturb a scene of a crime!' I intervened.

'No sir, of course not sir. I will see to it at once!' The constable departed immediately.

'Well done Watson, now the door!'

I pushed the door tightly shut and leant against it with my back. I was then surprised to see Holmes pick up Pike's notebook, tear out the front leaf and thrust the same into his inside jacket pocket. He replaced the book onto the table and joined me at the door. We slowly prised it open and once we were satisfied that the corridor was clear in both directions, we made our way stealthily towards the staircase.

'What about the description that you sent for?' I whispered as we headed for the front door.

'It was merely for confirmation, Watson. The identity of the porter is now clear to me,' Holmes replied inscrutably as he pulled on his coat and once more we went in search of a cab.

6

The Four-Handed Game

By the time that we had begun our return journey to Baker Street, the traffic had inevitably and dramatically increased. So much so in fact that at one point I was convinced that we would have made far better progress by simply walking back.

Nevertheless, this frustrating delay allowed me the time to request a summation from Holmes of his findings at Langdale Pike's club. For once and to my great surprise Holmes decided to acquiesce, without requiring any further persuasion.

'Even though you were privy to the majority of what I observed, I feel that it might be beneficial to both of us if I were to put into words the conclusions that I came to. It must have been fairly obvious that my examination of the windows revealed nothing at all. However the two sets of footprints, which I outlined upon the floor, showed me that the second party in the room, who was without a doubt Dave Bowman the supposed porter, was standing closer to Pike than would have been necessary under normal circumstances.'

'Why do you use the phrase 'supposed porter'?' I asked.

'Because, friend Watson, I am now in little doubt that Bowman will prove to be none other than the mandolin thief and Sophie Sinclair's assailant. I am familiar with Pike's boot size and the height of the other, as indicated by his boot size and the distance between them, matches exactly that of the perpetrator of the other two crimes. The space between both sets of prints would have been an ideal one from which Bowman could strike the fatal blow.

'We must not forget that Bowman was the last person to have seen Pike alive and my examination of the floor proved conclusively that nobody had entered the room until the morning, certainly not to remove Pike's dinner tray.'

'I understand, but surely Holmes, that space would hardly have provided enough room for a man to swing a sword.'

'Indeed not, Watson, but you are making one fatal assumption. How could Bowman possibly have hoped to conceal a sword from any potential passers-by, along the corridors of the club?'

'Of course, he must have used a knife! However, I can not, for the life of me, understand why one person would perpetrate a set of three crimes that were so disparate,' I declared.

'Ah, but you see Watson, I have now come around to your way of thinking. I have to agree that there does seem to be someone out there who is determined to attract my attention, regardless of the consequences. However, the reason for doing so is, for now at least, unknown to me.'

'Does that mean that you no longer hold to the theory that these crimes are a means of diverting you from your pursuit of the unholy trinity?'

'On the contrary Watson, that design is becoming more obvious to me with the execution of each successive crime. However, I am also more open to the persuasion that the person orchestrating these crimes has other, more personal motives behind them.'

I emitted a low whistle of disbelief and slowly lit my pipe.

'Now, however, we come to my *coup de grâce*,' Holmes proudly announced.

'You are referring, of course, to the sheet of paper that you removed so covertly from Pike's notebook. Obviously you have attached great importance to it; otherwise I am certain that you would have awaited the arrival of Gabriel's description of Bowman before beating your retreat.' Despite my efforts, I could not disguise a tone of censure from my statement.

'Watson, you might well disapprove of my removing an item of evidence from under the noses of the official force, but I assure you that my motives were not born of a desire to deceive them. It would be more appropriate to say that my intention was merely to save them from further confusion!'

I removed my pipe and was about to interject, when Holmes continued with great urgency.

'Before you protest at what you will no doubt see as a display of arrogance on my part, the names that were hurriedly written upon that sheet of paper will dissuade you soon enough.' Holmes flipped the offending sheet from his pocket and presented it to me with an extravagant flourish.

I was as dumfounded as the police would undoubtedly have been at the sight of the two names that Pike had hurriedly scrawled! There was that of Adele Fox, Sophie Sinclair's closest friend and confidante and Dr Marcus Harding, the surgeon of most dubious repute and a member of the Diogenes Club. However, my confusion was not to be lifted by Holmes, at least not for now.

'Your earlier point was certainly well made, Holmes,' I confirmed.

Holmes smiled at my admission, although there was nothing smug in his intention, for he was as confused as I had been.

'You will no doubt have observed the small spot of blood on the corner of the page? Well, that indicates to me that Pike had not only recognized the names and their connection to each other, but he had also attached great importance to them, since the clue he left for us was also his last act on this earth!'

'It looks like Pike's work was taking him along a similar path to our own, although the paths had never actually crossed,' I murmured thoughtfully, because any connection between the two, if indeed there was one, was a complete mystery to me.

'Hah! Baker Street at last and I should warrant that we will find two very impatient guests awaiting our arrival,' Holmes suddenly exclaimed as he leapt from the cab. 'Hurry, Watson!' he called, although I was still very much in the dark as to who these guests might have been.

By the time that I joined Holmes on the upper floor, our guests were already expressing their impatience and I was most surprised to find Inspectors Bradstreet and Lestrade on their feet and glaring angrily at Holmes. The only indications of Bradstreet's annoyance were his reddened face and bristling moustache. Lestrade, on the other hand, was altogether more vocal.

'Really Mr Holmes, anyone would think that two Scotland Yard detectives had nothing better to do with their time than to sit around in your rooms on the off chance that you might condescend to honour us with your presence!'

Lestrade's sardonic indignation reminded me of a time not so long ago, when Holmes and he were at loggerheads more often than not. Although their habitual mistrust of each other had evolved into a mutual respect over the years, it rarely took much for it to rear its ugly head once more.

On this occasion Holmes had actually added fuel to the fire, by totally ignoring the two police officers and he diverted his attention to two new wires that had arrived during our absence. Holmes tore them open feverishly and I could tell from his expression that both messages held exciting, if not entirely satisfying news.

He stuffed them both into his trouser pocket before attempting to placate the detectives, who were in the process of beating their disgruntled retreats.

'Gentlemen, I owe you both a thousand apologies for my lax time keeping, however the business at Langdale Pike's club took up more of my time than even I would have expected. The wires, on the other hand, should contain enough information of interest to persuade you both to remain.' Holmes invited them both to join him at the table, with his most charming of smiles and the enticement of our whisky decanter. Grudgingly Bradstreet and Lestrade relented and the four of us took to our seats with cigars and a glass of a very fine single malt.

'This is all very well Mr Holmes, but what exactly is the meaning of all of this tomfoolery?' Lestrade asked as he lit up his cigar.

Holmes' countenance assumed a gravity, the like of which I had never before witnessed. The effect that this had upon us was profound and striking and as a result, Lestrade was not able to raise another objection. Holmes stared solemnly at each of us in turn, but his gaze finally rested upon Lestrade.

'Inspector, I am afraid that we are dealing with something that is as far removed from 'tomfoolery' as you could imagine.' His tone of chastisement caused the inspector to swallow hard before he took a deep drink from his glass and Holmes was now assured that he had everybody's full attention.

'Before I go any further, I must have a solemn undertaking from each of you that not a single word of what you hear tonight will pass beyond these four walls, until such time as it becomes unavoidable. When that time does arrive, we shall all be fully aware of it, I assure you. To describe the dire consequences of such a betrayal would be impossible in the extreme.' Lestrade, Bradstreet and I all heartily agreed to comply and Holmes immediately relaxed somewhat. He lit his cigar and paused for a moment or two, while his thick smoke spiralled towards the ceiling and he slowly gathered his thoughts. Finally he placed his cigar in the ashtray and spread his hands out upon the table.

'Gentlemen, I must warn you now that you have agreed to join me in playing a most dangerous but critical four-handed game against a force, the scale of which neither of us can comprehend at present. I believe that Inspector Lestrade has some small understanding of the enormity of our undertaking, based upon his involvement at the conclusion of the unholy trinity affair and the death of Professor Ronald Sydney.

'However, it is only now, having been presented with so many dramatic cases within so condensed a period of time, that even I have some small grasp of the powers that now confront us. I assure you that, despite the illusion of his power, Professor Sydney was nothing more than a minion, a mere pawn, within a vast and hugely influential organization.

'Inspector Bradstreet, I see you raise a quizzical eyebrow — however, for the sake of your own wellbeing I beseech you not to underestimate the dangers that now threaten you! Remember that from the moment that you made your commitment to our cause, you shall no longer have the support of Scotland Yard at your disposal.

'Nobody, absolutely no one at all, can be privy to our work, until we reach the time when we have no other recourse. By then, of course, matters will have reached such a pass that we will need all the help that we can get.' Holmes smiled forbiddingly while he tried to construe the effect that his words had had upon each of us.

Evidently he was satisfied that the effect had been the desired one, for he now invited Lestrade to explain to Bradstreet the events and the exact circumstances of his involvement at the conclusion of the trinity affair. While Lestrade did so, Holmes picked up one of the newly arrived wires and took it over with him to his blackboard.

Obviously the wire must have contained a new anomaly that had been discovered by Denbigh Grey and in answer to my questioning glance, Holmes tossed it over to me once he had written the name 'Ulysses' large upon his blackboard. The wire read as follows:

Dear Mr Holmes,

I apologize for not having delivered this to you in person, but under the threatening circumstances that now confront me, I considered that a wire would prove to be a safer and more prudent method of getting this information to you, in the shortest possible time. By now you will have no doubt gathered that I have discovered another incongruity within the text, although it is one that may not appear obvious to you at first glance.

There is a reference to the ancient Greek hero Ulysses, during a passage that refers to the part that he had played in the fall and destruction of the city of Troy. The point being that Ulysses was a Latin translation of the Greek Odysseus which post-dated the time of Alexander by almost a hundred years! I hope that this information is useful to you and that it might bring *this awful business to a speedy conclusion. I shall await your best advice.*

Yours,

Denbigh Grey.

'This is all very well, but what can it possibly mean?' I exclaimed as I returned the wire to Holmes' outstretched hand.

Holmes had no other response than to pick up his chalk once more, in the hope that this new clue might aid him in his deciphering. By now Lestrade had concluded his summary to Bradstreet and Holmes indicated to me that I should take up the story from where Lestrade had left off.

The two detectives seemed to be both spellbound and astounded as I repeated the interpretation of recent events that I had previously discussed with Holmes, only omitting the names that Holmes had discovered upon the notebook of Langdale Pike.

They were both left speechless, although

after a moment or two and a further gulp of whisky, Bradstreet was the first to air his thoughts.

'It is certainly hard for me to reconcile any logic to the theory that each of these cases are somehow connected. On the surface, there is no common thread that binds any of them together. However, the facts seem to be inescapable.

'Harden was a member of the Diogenes and who can tell what dark secrets he took with him in death? The mandolin was stolen from the very scene of the conclusion of the Professor Sydney affair and even more remarkably, Sydney had been the very person who had earlier taken on one of the suspects.

'The motive behind the attack upon Sophie Sinclair is clear enough to me. These people appear to be ruthless enough to dispose of anybody who might present a threat to them, even with knowledge that they might have acquired inadvertently. I must confess, though, that the matter of Daxer's code and the death of Langdale Pike appear to be different matters altogether.'

Bradstreet concluded by lighting up his cigar and I have to admit that, by now, the atmosphere in our room resembled a dark and toxic mist.

Bradstreet's words had done nothing to move Holmes away from his blackboard. However, just as I had begun to mutter my own response, Holmes suddenly turned and with his eyes flaring with excitement, he produced the second wire.

'Gentlemen, I believe that I can forge the links that you are all grappling for. The lawyer who had achieved the early release of Theodore Daxer was none other than Sir Oswald Austin-Simons QC, the same man who had also ensured the liberation of Sydney's henchmen upon their return to London from Rome. You should also bear in mind that he is a long-standing member of the Diogenes Club. There is your link!' Holmes slammed the wire down upon the middle of the table in a most dramatic display that caused the decanter lid to fall onto the floor.

'Nevertheless, Mr Holmes, you have so far failed to present a connection between the death of Langdale Pike and the other cases,' Lestrade suggested mischievously.

Holmes glared at his former nemesis with a raised eyebrow and deep resolution.

'Before I can divulge that to you, I must humbly request a degree of tolerance and absolute discretion from all of you.'

Holmes searched the eyes of each of us in the hope of finding there his desired response. He was not to be disappointed, although Lestrade was noticeably more reluctant to acquiesce than Bradstreet and I.

'Excellent! Well then, I can reveal that I found this note upon Pike's desk at his club and I admit that I removed it from under the noses of two of Inspector Gregson's finest constables.' Evidently Holmes had decided to throw caution to the wind, in the hope of gaining the fullest cooperation from both gentlemen from Scotland Yard.

'Mr Holmes!' Lestrade exclaimed. 'Is there a reason for this blatant disregard of protocol? You do realize that the removal of an item of evidence from the scene of a crime is a prosecutable offence?' Lestrade paused for a moment of reflection before continuing; only now his tone was rather less aggressive.

'Was there a specific factor that prompted you to withhold this note from Inspector Gregson?' he asked with some trepidation, as if he already suspected Holmes' dark motive.

'He was not present at the time,' I explained with quiet diplomacy, although I noticed Holmes react impatiently to my inept and futile display of tact.

'For some reason I suspect that you would still have withheld it, even if Gregson had been there,' Lestrade speculated, while his nervous eyes darted back and forth involuntarily.

'Inspector Lestrade, I know Gregson to be a most thorough and methodical policeman, if not an inspired one and I found his actions at the scene of this crime to be irreconcilable to his normal ethic,' Holmes replied suggestively.

'Surely you are not trying to imply that a detective with Gregson's record and reputation can in any way be implicated in this catalogue of crimes?' Bradstreet asked incredulously.

'I am not implying anything, Inspector. However for Gregson to desert the scene of a serious crime at such an early stage and without having instigated a search for his principal suspect suggests that all was not as it should be. You must also bear in mind that I did demand complete discretion for a very good reason.'

'If we were to become certain that Gregson is in any way involved with this conspiracy, you can not seriously expect Bradstreet and I to remain silent upon the matter?' Lestrade blurted out.

'I not only expect you to, I demand it! The smaller the amount of suspicion that we arouse during our investigation, the more likely it becomes that this brother-hood will eventually betray themselves somewhere along the way. If we were to reveal Gregson's involvement at this early stage, it is hardly likely to remain a quiet affair and our adversaries will close ranks in a trice.' Bradstreet and Lestrade exchanged glances of agreement, despite harbouring some serious misgivings.

'Holmes, how deeply involved in this business do you suspect Gregson truly is?' I asked quietly.

'It is impossible to say, at this stage. However, these people are undoubtedly very persuasive when it comes to keeping their business out of the public gaze and they will go to any lengths to maintain their concealment. For now we shall assume that Gregson was left with little choice other than to turn a blind eye to their wrongdoings,' Holmes diplomatically replied.

'Even under these unnerving circumstances, Mr Holmes, you will retain our fullest cooperation, I assure you,' Bradstreet declared and Lestrade confirmed his agreement by nodding his head emphatically.

'Excellent! Now we may move forward, gentlemen, by analysing the names on Pike's note and trying to understand their significance.' Holmes placed the note upon the table and replenished our glasses from a decanter that was now half empty.

'Please note the small spot of blood on this corner. This undoubtedly indicates the great importance that Pike attached to their names, for the writing of them was surely the last action that Pike would ever take.'

In a weak, scrawled hand and with barely sufficient ink, Pike had written out the names of Adele Fox and Dr Marcus Harding. Although now familiar with the significance of both of these names and their involvement with the cases under discussion, the two detectives and I turned to Holmes for enlightenment, as neither of us could fathom any kind of logical connection between them.

For once Holmes was to disappoint us, for he appeared to be as nonplussed as the rest of us.

'Any link that does exist appears to be rather tenuous at best,' Holmes complained. 'Yet Pike used his dying breath to inform us of the importance of these names . . . ' Holmes began to tap his fingers upon the table in irritation and he sank into deep thought as he grappled with the problem.

'It appears that Pike was working upon much the same lines as we have been, although approaching from an entirely different angle,' I speculated quietly, although my words had evidently fallen upon three pairs of deaf ears.

A hushed and thoughtful silence had now fallen upon the room and the distorted butts of four cigars were now smouldering forlornly within the crowded glass ashtray upon the table. I for one had lost all track of time and it was only when the last glowing embers of our fire had begun to fall into the grate that we realized the lateness of the hour.

It was then agreed that Bradstreet would continue working on the case of the Venetian mandolin while Lestrade would pursue his investigation into the attack upon Sophie Sinclair. It fell to Holmes and I to solve the code of Theodore Daxer and Denbigh Grey together with the mysterious and savage slaying of Langdale Pike.

As I led the two detectives to the door, I could see that Holmes would abandon his work upon the blackboard for the night in exchange for a long vigil upon his chair by the dying fire. By the time that I had returned from showing out Bradstreet and Lestrade, Holmes was already well into his pipes and he sat there resolutely with his eyes tightly closed.

I knew from previous experience that it would be impossible to extract another word from Holmes until the morning and I quietly abandoned him to his long, lonely night.

7

The Diligent Undertaker

I was only too aware of the resilient properties that Sherlock Holmes' constitution possessed. Consequently, it came as no great surprise to me to find Holmes pouring himself a second cup of coffee at so early an hour, despite the sleep deprivation that he had subjected himself to the night before.

His greeting to me was surprisingly cheery and even though he would not be drawn upon the subject of our cases just yet, his conversation was quite amiable and he helped himself and me to liberal helpings of ham and eggs.

'So Watson, I perceive that you have every intention of visiting Miss Sinclair's sick bed at St Thomas' this very afternoon,' he stated in a rather matter of fact manner, whilst in the process of daubing some egg yoke from his lips with a napkin.

I was so taken aback by Holmes remarkable assertion that I replaced my fork upon my plate immediately, without having taken a single bite.

'Oh come along, Holmes, you really cannot possibly have any prior knowledge of that!' I protested, although I was already in very little doubt that he was just about to prove me wrong.

Holmes put his own fork down and then smiled at me mischievously while he lit a cigarette. He studied me closely for a moment or two and then smoked slowly and thoughtfully while he weighed up his conclusions.

'I suppose that you had assumed that because I had committed myself to deep meditation, just prior to your retiring for the night, I was unaware of the time?' I nodded my confirmation before Holmes continued. 'Nevertheless I was quite aware of the lateness of the hour, I assure you. I also recall that Wednesdays are the only day of the week on which you do not call upon your surgery, not even for a fleeting visit to collect your mail.

'Consequently, you usually take advantage of that by remaining within your bed for an extra hour at least, all the more so after such a late night. The notion of your starting the meal without having previously acquired a morning paper is normally abhorrent to you and yet . . . ' Holmes made an exaggerated examination of the table to emphasize the fact that I had done no such thing on this particular morning.

'Well, I suppose that you have made a couple of fairly obvious, but accurate, observations and embellished them with wild speculations,' I suggested with a smile.

Holmes was clearly agitated by my suggestion that he had guessed and continued to explain himself.

'Furthermore, when I see my friend clean shaven, on such a day, with his head bristling with pomade, I do not need to be the best consulting detective in the world to deduce that you have romance on your mind! You see Watson, although I am mistrustful and ignorant of such matters and I leave the fairer sex to your tender mercies, I still have the ability to recognize the contagion in others.' He smiled triumphantly.

I could not offer a single word in argument, for he had been absolutely correct on every point. Of course the fact that I could not control a blush of embarrassment gave Holmes all of the confirmation that he might otherwise have needed. However, his laughter was soon replaced with a more serious countenance when he began to contemplate the potential consequences of my paying Sophie Sinclair a visit.

'Nevertheless, Watson, I feel that under the current set of circumstances, it would be a grave error were you to carry out your plans,' he stated bluntly.

'Really, Holmes, and why would that be?' I asked, suspicious of his motives.

'Consider, Watson, that by now our adversaries, with all of the resources that they have at their disposal, will be fully aware of the fact that their attack upon Miss Sinclair had been an unsuccessful one. Lestrade has even allocated one of his best constables to keep watch over her, in anticipation of such an eventuality.

'Therefore, I think it would be unlikely that your visit to St Thomas' would go unnoticed and consequently you would not only be compromising your own safety, but also that of Miss Sinclair.' Holmes glanced briefly in my direction to ensure that his words had had the desired effect, before resuming his breakfast.

'I shall go and get a paper,' I grumbled, leaving Holmes in very little doubt that his advice had not fallen on deaf ears.

By the time that I had returned from my brief constitutional, Holmes had deserted the breakfast table and he was already at work upon his blackboard. As I no longer had an appointment to keep in the afternoon, I ensured that my breakfast was a long and leisurely affair and I took my second cup of coffee across to the fire with my pipe and paper.

Throughout this ritual of mine, I was constantly being reminded of Holmes' frustrations by the repetitious sound of chalk scratching upon the board, followed by repeated loud grunts of exasperation from Holmes followed by the inevitable swish of the duster wiping his redundant work away. Obviously, the longer that this process continued the more irritable he became. The grunts became louder and soon a small pile of broken pieces of chalk had begun to build up on the floor about his feet.

His failure to unlock the code was driving Holmes to despair and he retired from his work with a deep sigh of regret, as he slumped into his chair. He strummed his fingers repeatedly upon the arms of the chair and threw his tousled hair back from his brow, with violent sweeps of his hand.

'Surely matters cannot be as bad as all that,' I ventured, in an unsuccessful effort at easing his anxieties.

This was met by a further grunt from my friend and he jumped up immediately to begin rummaging for a cigarette and a match. I offered him one of my own and he snatched at it with a brief nod of gratitude. He seemed to swallow the smoke, as opposed to inhaling it and once it was done he retired to his room to set about his toilet.

He hollered down to Mrs Hudson for some hot water and it was while he was waiting for our landlady that he explained that it was not only his lack of success with the code that was so badly affecting his finely tuned nerves.

'You see, Watson, although I allocated the cases of Sophie Sinclair and the Venetian mandolin to Lestrade and Bradstreet respectively, I did so primarily to prevent them from obstructing our more critical work. There is less chance now of their stumbling across our path and scaring off the far bigger fish that we seek.'

I was appalled by the blasé manner in which Holmes was dismissing the attack upon Sophie Sinclair as something trivial and once he had returned from his room, I told him so.

'My dear fellow, perhaps you will now understand why I find it so necessary to divest myself from all attachment and emotion, when it comes to my clients and their little problems . . . ' Holmes responded, although I would not allow his last comment to pass without offering a retort.

'Little problem indeed — Miss Sinclair came within a hair's breath of losing her life!' It was rare for me to raise my voice when in the company of Holmes, but an admonishing glance from Holmes showed me that it had left him unabashed and that my emotional display had merely confirmed his point.

'It is not that I take the attack on your young lady lightly, Watson, but I am convinced that the perpetrator of both crimes is doubtless safely out of the country by now and our priority, therefore, has to be to establish the identity of his employer. Therefore, I am powerless to act until I receive a communication from either Denbigh Grey or Menachem Goldman, although preferably from them both.' Holmes' explanation had certainly diffused my anger and I offered him another cigarette, though against my better judgement.

Holmes now launched himself into a familiar pattern of pacing incessantly around our room, this broken only by an occasional cup of tea and frequent glances down the stairs in the hope of witnessing the arrival of the information that he awaited. It proved to be two tortuous hours before a wire finally arrived and once Holmes had torn it open, he was dismayed to discover that it contained nothing more startling than the date and time of Langdale Pike's funeral.

He was about to hurl this communiqué angrily into the fire, when a sudden change of heart caught his arm.

'You know, Watson, sometimes there is much to be learned from the congregation at a funeral. After all, it will doubtless be attended by a mixture of those who mourn the passing of the deceased and those who are glad to be able to confirm that the person has finally gone. I am certain that tomorrow's funeral will be no exception and that there might even be the additional element of those who merely wish to observe the other congregants, for reasons of identification.' Holmes passed the note over to me, so that I could make a note of the details that it contained.

Pike's funeral had been scheduled for

two o'clock the following afternoon at the Brompton Cemetery.

'It is certainly unusual for you to wish to attend such a gathering. I presume that it is for the same reasons that you have just described,' I suggested, although not for one minute had I contemplated the bizarre notion that Holmes was attending for reasons of sentiment!

'Exactly Watson. We simply cannot pass up the opportunity of being able to observe our enemies at work,' he confirmed excitedly.

'Are you suggesting that Pike's murderer might even be in attendance?' I asked, although one look at Holmes' expression told me that I had been somewhat wide of the mark.

'I think that would be highly unlikely, Watson, although his employers might have more than just a passing interest in the identity of Pike's mourners.'

'You are referring to members of the brotherhood, no doubt.'

'It is a distinct and enticing possibility,' Holmes confirmed and for a moment or two the news of Pike's funeral and the opportunities that it might be presenting us with seemed to alleviate Holmes' darkening mood, albeit temporarily.

However, it was not long before Holmes' aggravated pacing resumed and the names of Grey and Goldman could frequently be heard from under his breath each time that he returned from the hallway empty handed. Throughout the long hours that preceded Pike's funeral, Holmes turned aside every offer of food that Mrs Hudson presented him with and by the time that I decided to retire for the night, Holmes had become quite gaunt and grey.

The following morning came and went in much the same way and it was almost a moment of light relief when our old friend Gunner King finally arrived at our door with his cab.

The journey to Fulham was a slow and ponderous affair and we arrived at the cemetery and passed through the magnificent red brick archway with barely five minutes to spare. By the time that we had climbed down from the cab, a fine, chilling and penetrating rain had started to fall and we were glad for our umbrellas as we made the long walk down to the graveside from the neo-classically domed chapel.

My eyes were drawn not only towards the impressive outdoor cathedral but also to the sheer scale and splendour of some of the memorials that had lined our path. A dig in my ribs from Holmes' sharp left elbow reminded me of the true reason behind our attendance and I immediately turned my attention towards the other mourners.

The dank and dismal weather dressed the sombre occasion perfectly and although I had always disapproved of Pike and the scurrilous manner in which he had earned his living, I could not help but feel a pang of regret at his lamentably ill-attended final journey. In retrospect, I should not have been at all surprised at Pike's lack of friends. Holmes had informed me that his only living family member had been a long-estranged sister, Cornelia.

She was accompanied by her third husband, a rakish individual who went by the name of Victor Blake and their boorish teenage son, who had spent much of his time at the ceremony kicking large pebbles towards the graveside. Two tall and very well turned-out gentlemen, who had seemed far more interested in their own mutterings than the actual proceedings, two very elderly members of Pike's club and his long serving valet comprised the remainder of the assembly.

Holmes had been able to identify everybody to me, apart from the small group of preoccupied gentlemen, no doubt because of his many years of association with the flamboyant columnist. Consequently, their presence there provided us with the most intrigue. I could not help wondering if they had possessed any prior knowledge of the note upon Pike's desk and I was on the point of mentioning this notion to Holmes, when we discovered that the internment had been over almost before it had begun!

Without a solitary demonstration of grief or regret, the tiny entourage turned on its heels and made its way gratefully towards the shelter of the respective vehicles. Holmes and I were on the point of stepping into King's vehicle, when the very gentleman who had led the procession down to the grave stepped forward to introduce himself.

'Gentlemen please, if you would allow me to delay you for a moment or two, you might find my information of some little interest.' He spoke with a clipped and dulcet tone and a manner of assumed importance, which I found to be more than a little irksome. He was quite tall and exceptionally thin and when he smiled he revealed two rows of broken and discoloured teeth.

Holmes jumped down from the cab without a moment's hesitation and he invited me to join him in following the thin gentlemen's lead. He took us into a tiny, red-brick, four-roomed residence that was set just inside the cemetery's imposing north gate.

Once we were inside and being warmed by the cheery sound of a boiling kettle, our host bade us to take a seat while he introduced himself.

'My name is Nathan Joyce of Joyce and

Sons.' He made this announcement in a manner that implied that we would have had no difficulty in recognizing the name. He seemed disappointed to note that we had not. He expanded on this quite impatiently.

'Apart from being the cemetery super-intendent here, I am also the senior partner in what has long been regarded as the most respected funeral directors in London!'

'Ah, that Nathan Joyce, of course!' Holmes confirmed sarcastically.

Joyce appeared to be particularly put out by Holmes' offhand manner, but he continued to pour us out some tea, nevertheless. Joyce smiled expectantly while Holmes and I took our first tentative sips. They proved to be our first and our last attempts at sampling a drink that was, without doubt, the most toxic brew that I had ever tasted.

'I understand that you have some information for us,' Holmes reminded him, while he pushed aside his cup and saucer with an obvious air of disdain.

Joyce hurriedly removed the offending

crockery from the table and he eyed us both suspiciously, before deciding whether or not he should reveal his information to us.

'Ours is the third generation of Joyce's undertakers and consequently our company has become very well connected with the standard of people who demand ceremonial discretion at their funerals. Today's example had been, without a doubt, the most ill attended that I can recall. Sadly, it has also been the only one, that I can recall, where the arrangements have been put into place by the deceased's valet!' Joyce sat back suddenly, as if he had been startled and impressed by his own revelation. Again, he seemed disappointed to note that Holmes and I did not reciprocate.

Without so much as a by your leave, Holmes stood up sharply and made his way to the door.

'As fascinating as this insight into your tawdry little world has been, I feel certain that Dr Watson and I could be spending our time in a more worthwhile and productive pursuit!' Holmes declared as he opened the door.

Joyce jumped up at once and pulled the door closed once more.

'Oh Mr Holmes, forgive me, but I have more to tell you, much more.' Joyce revealed his teeth once again as he smiled apologetically.

'You see, I was merely trying to explain that the information I have for you has not been so easy to come by.' Holmes turned his face away from the undertaker's poisonous mouth and he looked down with contempt at Joyce's outstretched hand.

'I thought as much, Mr Joyce! You know, Watson, at this rate I shall become a bankrupt before this affair is brought to a satisfactory conclusion! Nevertheless, the value of your information is, as yet, to be determined.' Holmes released the door handle, but he refused to resume his seat.

'Of course, of course,' Joyce confirmed smugly. 'Well, I can tell you that I am also a student of nature and I could tell, from your expressions, that you were able to identify each member of the sorry gathering, save for the two stately

gentlemen who stood aloofly at the back,'
Joyce stated assuredly and triumphantly.

'In that case, Mr Joyce, you should also
be able to tell that I am not a man of
infinite patience! Now please continue,'
Holmes responded sharply.

Joyce had been clearly taken aback by
Holmes' brusqueness, and his air of
self-confidence rapidly fell away.

'Very well then, I can tell you with
absolute confidence, that the two gentlemen were none other than the distinguished
physician Dr Marcus Harding and Sir Oswald
Austin-Simons QC.'

To Holmes' annoyance I found myself
unable to contain my excitement at the
very mention of those two names in the
same breath. They had both been linked
with so many of our recent inquiries that
to find them operating in tandem
confirmed all of our worst fears. Holmes
tried to disguise my exclamation with his
own display of indifference. However,
even Holmes could barely refrain from
exhilaration when Joyce went on to
explain that he had also witnessed them
together at two other recent funerals that

he had conducted.

'I could not imagine why they would be in attendance at three such disparate funerals, but there you are. I see that you attach at least some value to my information, so I will tell you that the names of the deceased in question were Christophe Decaux and Mr John Vincent Harden.' Joyce smiled distastefully in anticipation of some reward, but he was more than a little dismayed when Holmes merely turned sharply on his heels and strode out of the tiny room, without offering the undertaker another word.

I found a couple of coins in my pocket for the disappointed undertaker and then immediately followed Holmes back to the cab. Holmes requested that King should divert to Scotland Yard on his way back to Baker Street and he insisted that we should travel in complete silence, while he attempted to collate his thoughts.

I waited with King while Holmes went about his mysterious business at the 'Yard' and it was not until we were safely back in our rooms at Baker Street and Holmes had lit a pipe that he decided to break his prolonged silence.

'I suppose that you would like some kind of explanation for our brief diversion?' he asked with a mischievous smile.

'Well, of course I would!' I declared emphatically.

'Oh Watson, I fear that I have placed your life in the gravest of danger. Indeed the lives of everyone connected with our enquiries are now under the gravest threat.'

'I was in little doubt of that and from the moment that I heard that Theodore Daxer was somehow involved, I had even expected it. However, danger is surely one of the prices that we have to pay in order to bring about justice, is it not?'

Holmes smiled proudly at me, through a plume of smoke, but I sensed that this was not all.

'I can assure you, Watson, that neither Austin-Simons nor Dr Harding were present at those funerals merely to confirm that their intended victims were indeed dead! They were trying to ascertain who else might have been close enough to each one of them and thereby pose a threat to their plans and organization.

'Do not forget that the cause of Decaux's death had been falsified by Harding, whilst Harden had also been a member of their club . . . ' Holmes stalled in mid sentence and I recognized a familiar facial expression of his that, more often than not, signified a sudden realization.

'So your mission at Scotland Yard was to organize some kind of police surveillance to ensure the safety of all those present at the funerals?' I speculated.

'It was indeed and I must say that I found our colleagues to be surprisingly cooperative on this occasion. However, I must confess that the death of Langdale Pike troubles me somewhat. Obviously Pike had been working on a story that had, at some point, dovetailed into our cases, albeit from opposing angles. Nevertheless, Pike had always been very discreet and cautious with his research and as far as I am aware, he had never been connected to the Diogenes Club, or to any of its members.

'Assuming that he had no knowledge of any of our investigations, it is inconceivable to me that he could have forged any kind of connection between the names within his notebook. It is fortunate indeed that Pike had the good sense and the strength to write them down for us before his death; otherwise we would not be having this discussion now. Despite the police precautions, I harbour grave fears for the safety of Adele Fox and I pray that they find her this night.' Before Holmes sank into a dark reverie, he assured me that Lestrade had agreed to intensify the cordon of protection that still surrounded Sophie Sinclair.

Despite this pledge, I cannot in all honesty claim that I retired to my room with any real peace of mind. My sleep that night proved to be a most fitful one and I could not have predicated the appalling manner in which the connection between those two names would be forged for us on the following morning.

8

The Whitechapel Ritual

I came down for my breakfast on the following morning, a little bleary eyed and with an unsettling sense of foreboding. Holmes had evidently retired from his fireside vigil at some point during the night and I pushed his door open gently to ensure his wellbeing before going out for the papers.

As I approached my usual stand I observed that an unusually large number of people had gathered around it. Furthermore, the vendor's call appeared to be provoking some kind of angry commotion amongst the throng. Normally I would have turned on my heels to seek the sanity of a corner shop. However, my curiosity was aroused and I was determined to discover the cause of this furore. I did not need to look any further than the fly on the vendor's billboard.

JACK THE RIPPER RETURNS
TO WHITECHAPEL

I did not have the time to dwell upon this startling headline, for the papers were selling quickly and I was determined to get one. I am ashamed to admit that I managed to barge my way through to the stand and I snatched out a copy without any by your leave! I hurried back to Baker Street, determined to share the news with Holmes immediately.

However, when I paused at the front door, I glanced further down the column and saw the name of the killer's victim. I was frozen to the spot when I realized that she had been none other than 'the up and coming young actress, Adele Fox'.

I tore up the stairs, calling out my friend's name as I arrived breathlessly upon the landing. To my disappointment, Holmes had yet to emerge from his room and my raps upon his door produced little response. Slowly the door creaked open and my dishevelled friend peered out at me in a state of annoyed confusion.

I did not offer him a single word of

apology or explanation, but merely shoved the paper's front page under his nose. His demeanour changed in an instant. He pulled his hair away from his eyes and grabbed the paper from me without ceremony.

'Watson!' he rasped.

A moment later he was pacing up and down in front of the fire, while he examined the offending article down to the finest detail and the final word.

'Watson, the manner in which the more sensational newspapers increase their sales is absolutely scandalous and irresponsible! As you will no doubt recall, their lurid reporting actually caused violent demonstrations on the streets, back in eighty-eight. I should not be at all surprised if they succeed in doing so again now.

'The very notion that Jack the Ripper has returned after an eight-year hiatus is utter poppycock and yet the gullible general public will, no doubt, lap this up and accept it as the absolute gospel truth.' Holmes tutted repeatedly as he hurled the repugnant journal to the floor in disgust.

He lit a cigarette and smoked it with great gusto while he weighed up the implications of this news. I retrieved the paper and tried to digest some of the finer details.

Apparently the police had only been able to identify the tragic Miss Fox by virtue of a number of letters and bill posts that she had carried within her bag. According to the preliminary reports, the injuries that she had suffered were the most horrendous that anybody had witnessed since or before those inflicted upon the Ripper's final victim, the tragic Mary Kelly. The wounds and mutilations were so similar to those found upon Kelly that the reporter stated that there was little doubt that this latest atrocity had been carried out by the same hand.

The body of Adele Fox had been found upon the steps leading up to the magnificent church of St Mary Matfelon and the discovery had created much disturbance and anxiety.

'Well, I must say the press seem to be doing everything within their power to create public hysteria,' I declared indignantly.

Holmes turned suddenly towards me, but I could tell from his wide-eyed glare that he had been barely conscious of my words. His mind was moving along a totally different path to mine.

'What can we surmise from the few scant facts within this report Watson?'

'Well, it seems fairly obvious to me that the newspaper is deliberately trying to convince its readers that Jack the Ripper has returned,' I replied.

'You are not convinced that he actually has?'

'As you said before, the notion is an utter nonsense! After all, it has been eight years since the last murder took place and the police are still no closer to identifying him. As I recall, there were a good many rumours and theories that were being bandied about for months after the grisly events. Some referred to a seriously disturbed Jewish butcher of Polish extraction, while another cited the artist Walter Sickert as a prime suspect.

'The most populist view, however, somehow linked a member of the royal family and an indiscretion of the most scandalous sort, with a Masonic doctor and a network of protective prostitutes whose secret led to their violent demise. All of these notions were deemed as plausible, but not one of them could ever be corroborated and the Ripper has since passed into a legend of the most lurid kind. The notion that he has now returned in order to mutilate a totally unrelated young actress is absurd.

'Nevertheless, somebody certainly seems to have gone out of their way to make it seem that the Ripper has indeed reappeared. I must say, however, that for the life of me, I cannot conceive of a notion that would explain why.'

Holmes stroked his prominent chin thoughtfully while his eyebrows became knotted to the point of contortion.

'Watson, this case is not yet clear to me. Assuming for a moment that you are correct and that the murder of Adele Fox was a mere replication of a Ripper killing, then the matter remains as to why.

Obviously we have the undeniable advantage over the authorities of knowing of the connection between Adele Fox, Sophie Sinclair, John Vincent Harden and the death of Langdale Pike.

'At first glance, the obvious conclusion to be drawn is that Harden's role within the Diogenes Club was more involved and complex than that of an innocent, naïve member. Indeed, it is not inconceivable that the knowledge he had held might have made his indiscretion with Sophie Sinclair seem like an extreme liability to the likes of Austin-Simons.'

'Hence, the attack upon Miss Sinclair and the murder of Adele Fox!' I exclaimed. 'However, why would they carry out these attacks in full public gaze if their intention was to maintain their society's discretion?'

'My thought exactly, Watson. It is almost as if they are trying to call attention to themselves, while going about the task of removing all possible threats to them. There is a certain contradiction here that belies the cleverness that they have thus far displayed. Perhaps there is another motive behind these crimes that has eluded us?' Holmes' voice tailed off while he lit his pipe and walked slowly over to the window.

'Do you mean to say that there exists another connection between each of these crimes?'

'I think it not unlikely, Watson.' Holmes drew on his pipe and gazed thoughtfully down upon the street below. 'Could it be . . . ?'

'What, Holmes?' I asked, but I held very little hope of receiving an immediate response. Consequently, I was very pleasantly surprised when he answered me immediately.

'For reasons that I am yet to fully understand, I believe that it is my attention alone that they are trying so hard to attract. You may well put this statement down to the arrogant nature that you frequently attribute to me, but you must consider the facts. Harden came to me with his peculiar little problem, knowing full well that I would uncover a good deal more than he had originally asked of me.

'Obviously Denbigh Grey's mystery is a different kettle of fish altogether, but everything else that has come our way of late has been expressly designed to lure me down a specific path of their choosing. They know only too well that even this epiphany of mine will not prevent me from continuing my pursuit of them.

'Consider this, Watson; they have carried out a theft from the very place where we had eliminated one of their leaders, executed a known associate of mine, in a manner with which we are only far too familiar and who was also making discoveries about them of his own design and now they have carried out this ritual slaying in Whitechapel! They have even chosen a church that bears the same name as the one that was so significant to us in Egypt![1]

'They seem to have no fear of the law; indeed, they may even see themselves as being above the law. I must admit that at times they do even seem to be! Nevertheless, their desire to entice me further towards the very centre of their conspiracy has made them bold, almost beyond the point of all reason.'

I let out a long, low whistle of disbelief while I considered Holmes' incredible theorizing.

'As always, your reasoning is flawless, Holmes, however it does not explain why they are so certain that you will be asked to participate in the investigation of this latest Whitechapel atrocity. After all, you were conspicuously excluded by the police back in eighty-eight, were you not?'

'Indeed I was, Watson, and that posed its own particular mystery in itself. At the time I put it down to the arrogance of just one man, namely the Commissioner of Police of the time, Sir Charles Warren. He dismissed the offer of my services in a most forthright and offhand manner, choosing instead to wallow in his self-induced, inert pool of darkness and ignorance, rather than accept the fact that his officers were simply not up to the task.

'Now however, in the light of some of the more creditable theories that surround the case, I am not so sure. Perhaps they were not so much afraid of my being able to identify the killer for them, but more that I might uncover some of the facts that they had rather remained hidden. After all, they surely recognized the fact that I was the only man in London capable of wresting the truth from within their labyrinth of lies.

'However, we can now put my ideas fully to the test. Are you up for a trip to Whitechapel, friend Watson?'

'Well of course I am! Allow me first to take every precaution.' Holmes smiled his agreement at once, knowing full well that I intended to fetch my trusty army revolver from my room upstairs. A moment later we were in a cab, bound for St Mary's of Whitechapel. To my surprise however, Holmes asked the driver to divert to the Diogenes Club, when we were already a good two miles into our journey.

I remained in the cab, while Holmes sprinted up the stairs to his brother's club and a moment later he flopped back into his seat, being both breathless and elated. Once we were on the road east once more, Holmes explained the reason for his spontaneous visit and also for his fulfilled excitement.

'Watson, I am sure that you will not be in the least bit surprised to learn that Sir Charles Warren had been a member of the Diogenes at the time of the Ripper murders.' I assured Holmes that I was intrigued to hear it but not at all shocked.

'Well perhaps this other piece of news might have the desired effect? Warren actually resigned from his office on the very night of Mary Kelly's murder! Furthermore, his resignation occurred prior to the discovery of the body and his decision to stand down had been so unexpected that nobody, not even his more senior officers, had entered the room of Mary Kelly until the news of his resignation had been made known to them. The officers on the scene of the murder actually delayed entry by over three hours, as they were expressly asked to act only upon receiving Warren's explicit and direct instructions. Three hours, Watson!'

'Surely his men could not have feared a

reprimand had they entered the room without Warren's say so? In heaven's name, Holmes, it was the scene of a murder after all!'

'You would think not, however Warren did seem to hold a very tight rein over all concerned with the Ripper killings. Even Inspector Abberline, a most able and respected police officer and a man who had been seconded from Scotland Yard specifically to head the Ripper investigations, tendered his resignation to Warren on more than one occasion because he considered the Commissioner's techniques and instructions to be far too restrictive and obstructive.'

I dropped my voice to a whisper.

'Holmes, surely you are not implying that Sir Charles Warren kept such a tight control because there were certain facts that he did not wish to have made public knowledge?'

'At this stage I am implying nothing. However, your speculation does certainly provide me with some food for thought.' With that, Holmes sank back into his seat with a lighted pipe and he smoked in total silence for the remainder of the journey.

By the time that we had arrived at White Church Lane, the huge crowds that had been reported had evidently dwindled away and those souls who had remained were being shepherded into a tight group by a small squad of police constables, well away from the blood-stained stairs of St Mary's. Holmes asked our driver to wait for us and then he made his way over to those very constables. They recognized Holmes at once and one of them ran off to call for their superior.

Evidently I had been more surprised than Holmes at seeing Inspector Gregson striding purposefully towards us, for my friend greeted him with a broad smile and a ready hand.

'Well, well, Inspector Gregson, what a pleasant surprise to find you here!' Holmes exclaimed.

Clearly Gregson did not reciprocate Holmes' sentiments, for he spurned Holmes' hand and asked his men why a member of the public had been allowed to approach the scene of the crime. He cast a disapproving eye in my direction, for I was already crouching over the bloodstains that had saturated those noble stairs. The body of Adele Fox had already been removed to the mortuary, but the rich darkness of the blood and the enormous area that it covered told me that a ghastly atrocity had taken place here. I walked back over to Holmes and Gregson.

'You seem to disapprove of my presence, Inspector. This surprises me, for you wasted no time in seeking my council over the death of Langdale Pike! By the way, have you had any success in locating the missing porter from Pike's club?' Holmes asked with an obvious mischievous intent.

Gregson was clearly embarrassed by this question, for he flushed and stumbled over a clumsy and apologetic reply.

'No, Mr Holmes, I am afraid that we have had no success so far, although I am inclined to agree with you that he is the only obvious suspect at the moment.'

'Perhaps the delay in instigating the search for him might have been at the root of the problem?'

Holmes seemed determined to cause the hapless detective as much discomfort as he could. It was obvious that Gregson understood the reasoning behind Holmes' line of questioning and he was also no doubt aware of the fact that it had been Holmes who had instigated the search for the porter in the first place.

'Very likely so, Mr Holmes,' Gregson replied in a more humble tone.

'I cannot help wondering if it would have been for the best if you had remained at Pike's club for a while longer than you did.' Holmes' persistence was clearly striking a distinct cord with Gregson, for he immediately adopted a more cooperative manner towards us.

'I am certain that you are correct, Mr Holmes, it was certainly remiss of me. Are you certain that you have completed your examination of the steps, Dr Watson?'

I nodded my confirmation and two of Gregson's officers immediately set to work removing the bloodstains with a bucket and some sponges. I tilted my gaze upwards and stared with wonder at the magnificent 200-foot spire that adorned the latest addition to London's skyline. St Mary's had only been completed a few years previously, but it had soon been adopted as an iconic landmark and place of refuge amongst the impoverished and deprived inhabitants of its parish.

I glanced across at Gregson and I could tell that Holmes' penetrating line of questioning had disturbed him greatly. Although his attitude at Pike's club was totally out of character for a man of his pedantic nature, I could not bring myself to believe that there had been anything malicious in his lack of foresight.

Perhaps he had simply been called away before he had been able to instigate a full examination of Pike's room? After all, Pike's notebook had been allowed to remain undisturbed on his desk, until the time of our arrival. Notwithstanding this, Holmes' probing had certainly had a positive effect and Gregson was now going out of his way to cooperate with us at every turn.

He offered to escort us around the exterior of the site, which had otherwise been cordoned off to the public. The church was bordered by Adler Street, White Church Lane and Whitechapel High Street, but our extensive patrol produced little result. The front door had remained locked throughout, so it had been decided that an examination of the interior would have been futile.

'I presume that you now wish to examine the sorry remains of Miss Fox at the Whitechapel Mortuary? However, I should warn you that her defilement will shock even gentlemen of the most hardened experience, such as yourselves.'

'Can you confirm the accuracy of the newspaper reports which stated that her injuries were an exact duplication of those suffered by Mary Kelly?' I asked, fully aware that Holmes was oblivious to our conversation, so engrossed was he with thoughts of his own.

'The resemblance between the two murders is uncanny, Dr Watson, that is for sure. It is almost as if the murderer has had access to either the police records or the mortician's report. Although, for the life of me, I cannot conceive of a way in which that might have occurred.' Gregson appeared to have been as perplexed as both Holmes and I were.

Just then Holmes finally decided to air the thoughts that he had so obviously been harbouring for the past few minutes.

'Gentlemen, is there a single doubt in either of your minds, that the murder was carried out right here upon the church steps?' he asked rather perplexingly.

'No, there is none whatsoever, Mr Holmes.' Gregson had been the first with a response and it had been an emphatic one. 'Once you have viewed the body you will be able to confirm for yourselves that the amount of blood we have found here corresponds with the nature and extent of Miss Fox's injuries. Furthermore, it would have been impossible to have moved the body, in its mutilated condition, without leaving further blood traces in the immediate vicinity.'

'I cannot find fault with a single word of Gregson's reasoning,' I confirmed.

'Very well then, there is really little more that can be learned here, come Watson!'

'Where are you off to now Mr Holmes, if I may ask? To the Whitechapel Mortuary, I should imagine.'

'With your kind permission, Inspector Gregson, I intend to visit the Norman Shaw building on the Embankment,' Holmes replied, although when he observed my confused expression, he added: 'It is the new home of the Commissioner of Police and I think that it would be more beneficial were I to view the files on Mary Kelly, prior to our examination of the body of the deceased. I take it that there are no plans to remove the body of Adele Fox from the mortuary in the immediate future, are there, Inspector?' Gregson confirmed that there were none and so, with a brief nod in the detective's direction, Holmes resumed his walk to our cab.

As I turned to follow him, I heard a sound that had been as familiar to me as it was disturbing. It was the unmistakable crack of a volley fired from a .303 Lee Enfield army rifle, of the type with which I had been issued during my service in the Afghan campaign.

My first instinct was to close ranks on my friend, to ensure his safety. I was gratified to note that Holmes had been equally concerned for my wellbeing and once we were both satisfied that the other had escaped injury, we sprinted back to the scene of the crime.

The sight of two of the constables stooped over a still and lifeless form upon the ground confirmed that neither Holmes nor I had been the intended target. I moved forward to examine the victim of this brief and sudden attack, only to discover that Inspector Gregson had suffered a serious, although not life-threatening injury to his right shoulder.

It was beyond my capabilities to remove the bullet without the aid of the necessary implements. Therefore, I bound up the wound as tightly as I could and advised the constables to order an ambulance without a moment's delay. Although the wound could be treated over time, I knew from hard-won experience that any damage inflicted by so powerful a weapon could easily result in the loss of a dangerous amount of blood!

Once I was satisfied as to the comfort of the inspector, I turned around to see how Holmes was reacting to this incident. To my surprise and dismay I discovered that my friend was nowhere to be seen! I turned this way and that and I even retraced our earlier steps by circumnavigating the entire building. Finally I sank down upon the steps and lit a cigarette, while I pondered upon my friend's current whereabouts.

Suddenly I heard his familiar voice ring out from somewhere above me.

'Watson, this is neither the time nor the place to relax,' he called out.

Holmes was sitting upon the edge of a low flat roof that served as an annex to the main building and which was attached to the base of the imposing spire. To avoid having to shout, Holmes sprang down to the ground beside me with the grace of a gazelle and then aired his thoughts and instructions in a whisper.

'Watson, as I watched you dress

Gregson's wound, I could tell at once that the bullet's trajectory came from a raised position. As I have just demonstrated, this particular roof also provides the means for an easy departure and this little discovery of mine confirms my hypothesis.'

Holmes opened up his clenched fist and he revealed a warm, empty shell from the spent bullet of a Lee Enfield rifle.

'Good heavens, Holmes!' I exclaimed.

Holmes hushed me with his hand placed over my mouth and he indicated that we should rejoin the constables that were still guarding their injured commander.

'Have you observed how the annex building falls fairly and squarely within the middle of the police cordon?' Holmes asked in an urgent whisper. We all nodded our confirmation.

'Then do you not see what this means? The would-be assassin must still be within a very close proximity of us and therefore, inside the cordon!' Holmes seemed to be exasperated at our lack of immediate comprehension; however we soon dispersed into four separate search parties of two, while the other officers ensured the safe departure of the members of the public that still remained.

As Holmes and I turned into White Church Lane, we assumed a low crouched position and our gradual advance was made with a wary vigilance. Holmes held his cane with the weighted handle by the base of the stem and his arm was crooked and ready to strike at a second's notice. I positioned myself a few paces ahead of Holmes and my revolver was cocked and steady.

We continued in this manner for what had seemed to be an eternity and as we turned the corner we were alerted by the sight of the tail of a black frockcoat flashing around the opposing angle. We quickened our speed at once, though without relinquishing our vigilance. A second later we threw our caution to the wind. There was no mistaking the sound of a powerful rifle releasing a second volley, though we could tell that its target was not moving in our direction.

Clearly the marksman was being approached by one of the other search parties and the sound of fast-moving heavy footsteps confirmed our instincts. A rifle shot echoed around the building once more and we made the next corner without a second being lost. We stood there breathlessly for a moment or two without betraying our position. However, a third rifle shot forced our hand and I raised my revolver as I realized our adversary would now know where we were.

A bullet immediately ricocheted from the wall next to me and it lightly grazed my cheek before thudding to the ground by my side. I gave not a thought to the innocuous wound, although we realized now that our mysterious enemy had managed to pin us down. Our only hope was that one of the constables would distract the marksman once again, thereby allowing me the time to get off a shot of my own.

After an agonizing ten minutes slowly passed by, we realized that this diversion was not to be immediately forthcoming. I was aghast when Holmes indicated to me what his intention was and I tried to restrain him with a look of alarm and a tug on his sleeve. However, Holmes was not to be so easily dissuaded and he rounded the corner with his cane held high.

He threw his weapon towards the man as a distraction. Holmes' perilous ploy clearly worked, for the man turned round suddenly to fire just as Holmes hurled himself to the ground. This gave me the opportunity I needed to fire first. I hit my target with surprising and unerring accuracy. He let out a cry and as it transpired, this was to be the last sound that he would ever make.

We rounded the corner and called for the constables to follow suit while we sprinted over to the body. The man had landed on his front, but Holmes and I were both dumbstruck once we had managed to turn him over to reveal his identity. It was none other than Sir Oswald Austin-Simons QC!

'Good heavens!' I exclaimed, for I was horrified at the thought of a man from such an eminent position being so corrupted by the forces that were behind him and his nefarious activities.

If I had been horrified, then Holmes had been as crestfallen as I had ever seen him. He had turned away from the sight of the fallen barrister and then lit a cigarette while he gazed forlornly up at the magnificent spire, almost as if seeking some kind of divine inspiration.

It was inconceivable for me to believe that a man such as Holmes was feeling any kind of remorse at the death of Austin-Simons. I remembered that he had once stated that there was nothing worse than a man of intellect succumbing to the lure of crime. Consequently I was convinced that there had been another reason behind his distraught manner.

'What course of action would you now advise? Do you believe that Austin-Simons had been Miss Fox's murderer?' I asked, in the hope that Holmes would now reveal the reasons for his melancholy.

'I do not believe Austin-Simons to be her killer, but I do believe that a good number of vital answers have died with him!' I was aghast to observe that Holmes could barely contain his disappointment at the fact that my shot had proven to be a fatal one. He turned away abruptly from his reverie and looked upon me with a great intensity.

'Are you suggesting that perhaps I should have allowed him to shoot you, for the sake of a potential fount of information?' I asked sarcastically.

Holmes' manner immediately warmed appreciably and he almost managed a smile as he replied.

'No, of course I do not, Watson. As always, I am fully appreciative of your most timely intervention, although I do believe my regret to be totally understandable. Austin-Simon's demise will certainly increase the amount of work that we have yet to do.' Holmes slapped me upon the shoulder and then encouraged me, in a most gingerly manner, to return my revolver to the safety of my pocket.

Once we were satisfied that Gregson was safely on his way to the nearest infirmary, Holmes and I persisted with his original intention of a trip to the Victoria Embankment and the Norman Shaw building. Once we were on our way, I asked Holmes to explain why he considered Austin-Simons to be innocent of Adele Fox's murder and the reason for the barrister's attack upon Inspector Gregson.

On this occasion, Holmes was not slow in coming forward with his explanation.

'Watson, if the reports that we have read are to be believed and the abominable rites that were carried out upon Miss Fox's body are in fact a mirror of those carried out upon the victims of Jack the Ripper, then I think we can be certain that the perpetrator must have possessed more than just a passing knowledge of medical surgery.

'Despite his other dubious talents, I do not believe Austin-Simons to be a man of medicine. Furthermore, even if he had miraculously discovered these new abilities, he would be foolhardy indeed were he to remain at the scene of his crime for as long as he did. No, I believe that the search for the killer must take us along an entirely different path to that.

'As for his attack upon Inspector Gregson, I believe that if either you or I had happened to have come within the sights of Austin-Simons, he would have displayed a similar lack of compunction in bringing us to the same sorry pass. Evidently and in spite of any misgivings that he might have harboured, Gregson has come under the influence of the very group of people that we seek. His uncharacteristic display of incompetence at Langdale Pike's club is ample evidence of that!

'I am of little doubt that they had come to question the strength of their influence over Gregson, being fully aware of the sterling service that he had previously always given in the pursuit of justice. Consequently, the very sight of him in a cordial discussion with the two of us prompted them to take an immediate and drastic form of action, lest he betray some of their secrets.

'Remember Watson, these people cover their tracks in a most thorough and ruthless manner and any misgivings that they might have been harbouring over his tenuous loyalty would have resulted in him coming under constant surveillance. The fact that they have missed their mark and lost one of their staunchest allies into the bargain can only result in their redoubling their vigilance. Remember also, dear friend, that they are now running out of targets!'

'Whoever 'they' might happen to be,' I muttered to myself. 'With the demise of Sydney, Harden and now Austin-Simons, we are also running out of options, old fellow, perhaps in more ways than one.' I patted my pocket in the hope that the shape of my revolver would be enough to give me renewed strength and fortitude.

I glanced over at my friend in anticipation of a positive response. However, he was staring straight ahead, his eyes shining with a steely intent and oblivious to my dilemma.

9

The Covert Files

Upon reaching our destination, I lost no time in alighting from the cab. However, when I turned around in expectation of finding my friend standing by my side, I was surprised to see that he had decided instead to cross the road towards the river.

Holmes was leaning against one of the newly installed 'Mabey' lamp posts and he was in the process of lighting his pipe in a most leisurely fashion when I went across to join him.

'Has our unannounced appointment with the Police Commissioner suddenly lost its urgency?' I asked, feeling that Holmes' languid manner somehow belied the magnitude of our mission.

He waved his pipe back and forth as if tracing the line of the grey, pulsating river. The wind had picked up somewhat and the eternal Thames had now risen to a full and throbbing tide.

'You know Watson, it is not an inconceivable notion to observe the manner in which the behaviour of a grand old river, such as the Thames, might mirror the life of a man. Born as a bright and bubbling mountain spring, ever increasing in size and vitality as it grows into a burgeoning stream, slowly maturing into an expanding and vibrant river and then tiredly emptying out into a dark and murky estuary, having expended the last of its power and energy.

'Man, however, has the ability to change his course and therein lies the eternal problem that is faced by each one of us at some point in our lives: that of choosing the correct course to take. A river faces no such conundrum and therefore it is not so hard to envy its passive and charted existence.' Holmes paused to pull on his pipe and I realized that this brief philosophical interlude of his was but a prelude to the enormous and hazardous undertaking that lay before him.

Without uttering another word and with a fresh purpose and determination in his actions, Holmes emptied his pipe out against the side of the ornate lamppost and strode across the street towards our objective.

The Norman Shaw complex was comprised of two identical, monolithic red-brick buildings that gazed forbiddingly out towards the river. One of these was still under construction and the constant noise made by the various mixers, hammers and drills was quite deafening. We arrived at the porter's desk within the completed building with a sense of relief, as if we had found a place of refuge from the grimy and repugnant machines next door.

We sprinted up the two long flights of stairs that led to the commissioner's office, but we were then brought to an abrupt halt by an austere and imposing secretary, perched imperiously behind a huge rose wood desk. Her tightly bunned hair and horn-rimmed spectacles projected an air of authority that was unmistakable and irresistible.

Despite Holmes' most charming smiles and persuasive entreaties, the matronly woman steadfastly refused to show us through to the Commissioner until she was certain that he had completed his other business of the day. Although she clearly recognized our names, she resented the effrontery of our presenting ourselves without having previously made an appointment!

Holmes found this delay too much to bear and he began pacing ceaselessly in front of the desk, grumbling all the while as he went. Finally, our agony was relieved when the 'other business of the day' turned out to be none other than Inspector Lestrade making his report and he was quite amused to observe our dilemma and frustration as he made his way towards us.

'I am sure that the Commissioner will find time for you now,' he sneered and sure enough, not a moment later, we were invited to go through.

I must admit that, because of the interminable length of time for which we had been kept waiting, I feared that the reception we were about to receive would prove to be as frosty as the one proffered by Sir Charles Warren, eight years previously. Fortunately my misgivings were soon proven to be totally unfounded.

'Mr Holmes and Dr Watson, I must offer you both a thousand apologies for having kept you waiting for so long. That popinjay Lestrade certainly seems to enjoy the sound of his own voice.'

General Sir Edward Bradford was certainly not a man for standing on ceremony. He greeted us with a broad, open smile and he sprang around the side of his enormous desk with a sprightliness that belied his years. His handshake was firm and enthusiastic and Holmes and I were made to feel totally at ease as he waved us into our seats by the enormous fireplace. Bradford pulled over a chair of his own and he joined us there once he had placed an order for a tray of tea.

Bradford had retained the bearing and physique of a military man, despite being well into his sixties and we would subsequently discover that he had served with great distinction and bravery during his long tour of duty out in India. His hair was silver, but distinguished and his profuse facial hair shone out from his genial, ruddy complexion.

While we waited for our refreshments, Bradford spoke at some length and with great passion upon the subjects of his two favourite projects, namely the introduction of motorized taxi cabs upon the streets of London and the setting up of an independent fingerprint department under his jurisdiction. I was not surprised to note that Holmes certainly shared Bradford's enthusiasm for the latter.

Nevertheless, once the tea things had been removed and we had each smoked one of Bradford's most excellent cigars in an appreciative silence, his manner assumed a sudden gravity that was almost disconcerting. He jutted his head towards ours, to form a tight triangle and he dropped his voice to a barely audible whisper. He explained this abrupt alteration to his behaviour in an instant.

'As I am sure that you have already deduced, one cannot afford to be too careful nowadays. Every wall seems to have a subversive ear and it is becoming increasingly difficult to judge as to whom one can completely trust. I take it that you have come to me regarding that awful business in Whitechapel?'

'Indeed we have sir,' I confirmed.

'As you have already no doubt surmised, the press are doing everything within their power to ensure that the public believe this heinous crime to be the work of Jack the Ripper. I, on the other hand, will take whatever measures I deem to be necessary to subvert this odious theory.

'After all, the last thing we want, in these volatile times, is a further display of public fear and the consequent unrest upon our streets that this might cause. There will be no repetition of 1888 during my tenure, I can assure you!'

'That is a very fine speech indeed, Commissioner; however I do recall that your predecessor was also a most eloquent orator. His actions, on the other hand, left much to be desired!' I was surprised that Holmes had chosen to adopt such an aggressive and cynical tone with our genial host, bearing in mind the level of cooperation that we required from him. Thankfully, Bradford seemed to be unabashed by Holmes' attitude.

'Mr Holmes, I can assure you that I am not Sir Charles Warren, although I can readily understand your lack of confidence in men of our position. As I recall, your services were dispensed with in a most offhand manner at the time of the previous attacks.' Holmes nodded his confirmation.

'I have my own ideas as to the reasons for Warren's dismissal of my services, but can I be certain that you are the man to whom these can be revealed?'

'The worst of crimes warrant the best of detectives, Mr Holmes. What do you need of me? My resources are completely at your disposal and I can guarantee you my fullest cooperation!' Bradford appeared to be as sincere as he was emphatic and not surprisingly, Holmes had clearly been moved by Bradford's compliment.

Holmes slowly stood up and he lit a cigarette by the open window.

'I would rather not show my hand until I have delved deeper into the matter and assured myself of the facts.'

'I am happy to proceed on that basis,' the commissioner agreed with a smile.

'I shall require full access to every document, photograph and file that was produced by the investigators into the Mary Kelly killing,' Holmes stated with determination while turning away from the window.

'I shall have them brought up to my office this very minute. You might even use my desk for their perusal, where you shall be completely comfortable and undisturbed,' Bradford assured him.

'Can I also assume that my friend here, Dr Watson, will be able to view the body of Adele Fox at the mortuary and view the mortician's notes without delay and hindrance?'

'I shall send a note of authority across at once and my carriage will be at his disposal.'

Now it was Holmes' turn to smile.

'Well Commissioner, perhaps we shall get to the bottom of this matter after all.

Who knows, perhaps we might even be able to finally close the original Ripper files to everyone's satisfaction.' Holmes rubbed his hands together excitedly at the prospect while Bradford began to write his notes.

Commissioner Bradford was as good as his word and a few moments later I was being whisked along to Whitechapel in a very fine brougham indeed, leaving Holmes to paw hungrily at the monumental mound of files that had suddenly appeared upon the Commissioner's desk.

I must admit that the prospect of my mission was not one that I viewed with a great deal of enthusiasm. I still retained a vivid recollection of the reports into the death of Mary Kelly and despite my vast experience of the travesties that man was capable of inflicting upon his fellow human beings, I must admit that the idea of viewing the mutilation of Adele Fox filled me with a certain dread.

The Coroner's Mortuary of Whitechapel turned out to be a small, single-storey, red-brick building that bore more than just a passing resemblance to a tiny church, although without the spire. It seemed strange and anachronistic to think that such a quaint and tranquil looking building could contain the atrocities that I knew were kept behind its walls.

The head mortician was the epitome of enthusiastic cooperation and he even offered me a cup of tea to drink while I was going through his gruesome files! Finally, I was led through to the mortuary itself and I could hardly contain my revulsion as the tray containing the remains of Adele Fox was pulled out in front of me.

It is impossible for me to find any words that will not offend my reading public, which could accurately describe that vision of human desecration. I could not reconcile the violence that had been perpetrated upon this unfortunate young woman with any semblance of normal behaviour. I readily confess to having shed a tear or two, not for the victim but for the notion that any human being could carry out such an attack upon another.

There was no part of the unfortunate woman that had been left undisturbed and it was, therefore, impossible for me to compare the disfigured corpse before me with a photograph of her that the mortician had shown me just a moment before.

Yet, the mutilations were clearly not the result of the mindless hacking perpetrated by a thug armed with a surgical blade. Great skill and accuracy had been employed in the intricate removal of some of her organs and I was left with the horrifying conclusion that the attack could only have been carried out by a man of medicine.

I had seen enough and I asked for the removal of the body without a moment's delay. I remained alone and motionless within the middle of the empty room and my reeling head made it impossible for me to take a step towards the door. Finally the mortician returned with a large glass of brandy and after a sip or two of the soothing drink, I finally felt able to return to the brougham.

I asked the driver to pull over while we

were passing the first available open space, so that I might clear my head with a brisk walk and a sharp intake of cool, fresh air. Although my brief diversion certainly had the desired effect, I knew, in my heart of hearts, that the vision that I had seen that afternoon in Whitechapel would stay with me for the rest of my days.

I returned to the Embankment in a most sombre mood and even the sight of Holmes brandishing the files with a flourish of great excitement and, dare I say, not a little pleasure, did nothing to alleviate that frame of mind.

'We have our case!' he declared and I could tell by the expression on Bradford's face that Holmes' conclusion was one with which the Commissioner heartily concurred.

Nevertheless, neither Holmes nor Bradford were completely oblivious to my plight and without a moment's hesitation, Holmes offered me his tobacco and placed a comforting hand upon my shoulder. I found it impossible to describe my experience in

Whitechapel in any great detail, but I soon realized that it was my duty to gather my thoughts together and express them coherently.

'When I read the headlines of this morning's papers, I could not believe for one second that a serial killer, who had been dormant for over eight years, would suddenly reappear merely to snub out the light of an aspiring young actress.

'Potentially she might well have been in possession of information relevant to several cases that we have been working upon of late, but could that be the reason behind a killing that was surely going to attract a good deal of attention in the public press? The idea of that seemed to be ludicrous in the extreme. However, the other explanation, that they were merely attempting to attract the attention of Sherlock Holmes, appeared to be even more so.

'Gentlemen, I have to tell you that, having examined the medical reports from the original killings and extensively viewed the lamentable remains of Adele Fox, I was wrong from the beginning.

There is now no doubt in my mind that the killer of Mary Kelly and that of Adele Fox are one and the same!' I lit up my pipe and peered over the bowl towards my companions, half expecting a torrent of derision to cascade upon me from both directions.

To my surprise and dismay, this was not to be forthcoming.

'I am very much relieved to hear you say so, old fellow, for that is the very conclusion that I have now come to, although by a completely different route.' Holmes was still holding the files and I realized at once that the secret behind this epiphany of his lay within the brown and worn sheets of paper that they contained.

I looked across at Commissioner Bradford and he was nodding sombrely, in total agreement with my friend.

'The facts are indisputable, Dr Watson, although the motive behind the killing is still very much an oblique question.'

'Of course that is another factor that binds the two cases together. However, if we consider the least bizarre notion that was circulating at the time of the original killings, that a dark secret of a member of the aristocracy was being shielded by his fellows from the public gaze, then one or two of the anomalies that lay within these files suddenly make more sense,' Holmes explained excitedly.

He rummaged chaotically through the papers until he found what he had been looking for with a cry of triumph. He thrust the sheets under my nose and smiled expectantly while I read through the sentences that Holmes had under-lined with a pencil. His discoveries had left me quite breathless and Holmes continued with his explanation before I had even had the chance to voice my reaction.

'Once you realize the implications of this report, it is quite easy to understand the sense of public outrage that mani-fested itself at the time. Why would the post mortem on Mary Kelly have been carried out in Shoreditch instead of the more obvious Whitechapel Mortuary, unless there was something that the authorities wanted to keep hidden from the public[1]? There was clearly something more profound about the killing of Mary Kelly, because all of the other examinations had actually and understandably taken place in Whitechapel.

'The flames of anger upon the streets of the East End were stoked up still further once it was revealed that the inquiry into the Kelly murder was concluded and closed in less than twenty-four hours! Even an investigation into a commonplace death takes longer to complete than that!' Holmes tried to quell his agitation with a cigarette.

'That is outrageous!' I exclaimed.

'Sir Charles Warren certainly did his best to suppress some vital information,' Bradford quietly confirmed, although he was clearly taking no pleasure from the fact that his predecessor had behaved so deplorably. 'The contents of these files are testament to that. However the pressure that was being brought to bear by the public eventually proved inescapable and he had no choice but to resign.'

'Did he not resign before the killing of Mary Kelly?' I asked. 'If that is the case, the scandal created by the inadequate inquiry into her death would have been totally irrelevant to him,' I suggested.

'No Dr Watson, he had merely tendered his resignation, never really supposing that it would have been accepted. Despite his powerful friends and allies, he soon realized that for his own safety, he simply had to go,' Bradford quietly explained.

'Now I understand. So I suppose that the only question remaining is the one that has been on everybody's lips for these past eight years. Who was Sir Charles Warren actually protecting?'

'I am afraid that is something that we are never likely to discover. Warren and his confederates have been entirely successful in ensuring that. Nevertheless, the identity of the actual killer has proven to be somewhat easier to ascertain.' Holmes could barely suppress a smile of self-satisfaction once he had noticed the look of astonishment upon my face.

'Oh come along, Holmes!' I protested. 'You simply cannot expect me to believe that, after eight years of speculation and investigation, you have solved the mystery of Jack the Ripper in a single afternoon?'

'It is actually somewhat less than that, old fellow. However when you consider the obvious advantages that we have had over our predecessors, it is not so impossible to believe. Besides, we must not forget that we are not the first to achieve this feat, although our forerunner was not aware of the magnitude of his discovery, nor had that been his intention.'

My head was now spinning with bewilderment, for I had absolutely no idea as to whom Holmes was referring. Thankfully, Holmes was not slow in recognizing and then relieving me of my predicament. He held up a small page of notepaper that I immediately recognized, but this did nothing to make matters any clearer to me — quite the contrary in fact.

'Watson, I have decided to take Commissioner Bradford fully into our confidence, for that is our only hope of ever defeating the Bavarian Brotherhood. Consequently I have shown him the note from Langdale Pike and explained to him its significance.

'We have discovered that the extent of the injuries to the Ripper's victims were only made known to the public in the first four of the cases. The horrific natures of Mary Kelly's injuries, however, were known to only two men and to them alone! These were Dr Thomas Bond, who had actually conducted the post mortem examination and his assistant, who had been taking Dr Bond's notes. Bond's career contained no blemishes whatsoever and both his character and integrity are beyond reproach. His assistant, however . . . '

'Good heavens Holmes, it was Dr Marcus Harding!' I finally declared.

'Exactly Watson, and the implications of this are clear, are they not?'

'Well it certainly shows that the brotherhood was actively covering up its traces as far back as eighty-eight,' I stated with confidence.

'A good deal further back than that, I would say. After all it must have taken them considerably longer than eight years to construct a society as complex as theirs. To think that we previously thought that the elimination of Professor Ronald Sydney was going to be the conclusion of the matter! We have barely scratched the surface, Watson, and we can be certain that the likes of John Vincent Harden and even Dr Harding were acting as nothing more than mere minions.' Holmes was clearly much moved by the enormity and the gravity of the task that still lay before us and I shuddered involuntarily while he spoke.

'I presume that our first action will be to proceed against Dr Harding? After all, he is responsible for the deaths of at least two innocent young women, not to mention the fact that he was protecting someone of considerable importance and power, whose dark deeds we can only speculate upon,' I suggested.

'Dr Watson, even though I can promise you both that all of my resources will be at your disposal from this moment on, I will still only act within the framework of the very law that I have sworn to uphold. You must try to understand that the evidence against Dr Marcus Harding, as damning as it is, is nothing more than circumstantial. There is not a court in the land that would rule against him, given the facts that we would be able to present to them. Indeed, it would, in all probability, do our cause more harm than good were we to move to prosecute him,' Bradford explained, although with some obvious regret.

'This is absolutely outrageous!' I exclaimed.

'Indeed it is, Doctor, but I have to agree with the Commissioner. Nevertheless, I am sure that we can take measures to ensure that Harding never practises medicine again. Besides, who can tell what fate might befall him were he to suddenly lose his importance to the brotherhood?' There was something quite disturbing about Holmes' speculation.

'I will do all that I can to bring about his disgrace. However, were you to discover any further, more tangible evidence that can be used against him, I assure you that every legal device at my disposal will be brought to bear against him!' Bradford assured us with not a little passion.

'Then that will have to suffice for now,' Holmes stated while rising to take his leave. Once again Bradford shook us both warmly by the hand and there was something in their exchange that gave surety to me that both Bradford and Holmes were determined to bring Harding to the dock.

After all, there was every reason to believe that Dr Marcus Harding was indeed the man to whom history and legend had given the name of Jack the Ripper.

10

The Bavarian Recluse

While it had certainly been most gratifying and reassuring to note that, in Commissioner Bradford, there was at least one person of influence and authority who had not, as yet, been corrupted by the forces behind the Bavarian Brotherhood, it had also been disappointing to realize that Sherlock Holmes could never be revealed as the man who had solved the case of Jack the Ripper.

Although I fully understood the reason for this gross injustice, I found it galling to have to accept the notion that a man such as Dr Marcus Harding was still able to enjoy his liberty. Although they would undoubtedly prove to be unacceptable to a court of law, I found the evidence of Langdale Pike's note and the fact that Harding had been present at the examination of Mary Kelly's body to be irresistible and I told Holmes so during our journey back to Baker Street in Commissioner Bradford's brougham.

Despite the positive reaction that we had received from Bradford, I could not fail to notice that Holmes had fallen into one of his darkest moods. He had not uttered a single word throughout the entire journey and he could not even rouse himself from his malaise in order to smoke. I felt that I understood the reason for his latest emotional descent.

'Really Holmes, I will not allow you to blame yourself for the horrid fate of Adele Fox. You implored the police to do their utmost in locating her and no man could have possibly done any more than you.'

Slowly Holmes raised his eyes from the floor of the carriage and he allowed himself a brief glimpse at my own. Perhaps he had been trying to ascertain the degree of my sincerity? Evidently he had been convinced by what he saw.

'Perhaps you are correct, Watson — maybe there was little more that I could have done. Yet despite all of my efforts and clever deductions, this brotherhood always appears to be one step ahead of me. Even when we were on the cusp of questioning one of their leading lights, you were forced into eliminating him in order to spare my life. You did well, my friend, and I shall forever be in your debt,' he added in earnest.

'It was no more than you would have done for me, under the circumstances,' I responded.

'Perhaps, however I could not assure you of my being able to achieve the same degree of accuracy.' I was relieved to see Holmes achieve something akin to a smile and I attempted to encourage him further.

'When we get back to Baker Street we will be able to set our plans in motion once more. Do not forget that we now have the full weight of Commissioner Bradford behind us — and who knows what Menachem Goldman might yet discover? In any event, another elite member of the brotherhood has been removed from our path.'

Holmes was still not convinced, however.

'This brotherhood is like the Hydra, Watson, it seems as if the instant we cut off one of its heads another one grows in its stead, just as Professor Sydney had predicted.'

'Ah yes, but he had not anticipated the alliance that we have now formed with two of Scotland Yard's brightest lights!' Holmes knew that I was referring sarcastically to Inspectors Bradstreet and Lestrade and he finally managed to laugh, albeit at their expense.

Our moods were certainly much lighter by the time that we had reached our rooms, although our jovial display was curtailed somewhat by the sight of a nervous and edgy Denbigh Grey standing by the window. The uncertainty that had hung over him for so long was taking its toll and his relief upon our return was excessive but entirely understandable.

'Oh Mr Grey, please take a seat and calm yourself for heaven's sake! We are not your enemies.' Holmes placed a reassuring arm around the little man's narrow shoulders and guided him towards a chair by the fire.

'Now explain to us, please, why you have forsaken the safe recourse of sending me a wire, for the more reckless challenge of coming here in person?'

'The explanation for that is a simple one, Mr Holmes. I have discovered a fourth anomaly within the text, but I have decided that a personal delivery might speed up the process of bringing this awful business to a safe conclusion. My nerves are being stretched to the point of snapping in two!' Grey explained with passion.

'That is entirely understandable, Mr Grey,' I confirmed quietly with a smile.

Holmes was clearly irritated by my attempt at reassuring our nervous client.

'I would say the exact opposite, Mr Grey, for in coming here today you have surely jeopardized a satisfactory conclusion to this entire affair! Now would you please explain the nature of this fourth anomaly?'

Grey was so upset by Holmes' rebuke, that it took him a full three minutes before he was able to formulate his next words coherently.

'I must admit that my latest discovery is a far more obscure and subtle one than any of the others, so far. Indeed, I would be most surprised if anyone other than a most learned scholar of Greek history would have even been aware of it.

'The passage in question refers to the violent death of Nearchus, who had been the admiral of Alexander's fleet and one of his closest confidants . . . '

Grey paused in his account because Holmes had obviously and inexplicably lost all interest in the remainder of Grey's explanation. He had rushed over to his blackboard and without a moment's hesitation, he grabbed his rag and wiped off all traces of chalk from the board with wide and violent sweeps. Grey was as dumfounded as I had been by Holmes' strange reaction, but he continued bravely nonetheless.

'The point being, Mr Holmes, that records show how Nearchus was actually present at the side of Alexander's bed at the time of his death!' Grey concluded with a flourish; however, for all the interest that Holmes had shown, he really need not have bothered.

'Really Holmes, this is intolerable behaviour. You have obliterated all traces of your hard work, without so much as a word of explanation, neither to Mr Grey nor to me!' I exclaimed in exasperation.

Holmes had been totally oblivious to Grey's conclusion and he sank back into his chair wrapped in his own deep thoughts. Grey was clearly lost for words and he looked anxiously towards me for some kind of justification.

I had none, of course, but Grey steadfastly refused to be denied.

'Mr Holmes, I simply will not be put off, nor will I leave here today until you have outlined to me your plan for bringing this matter to an end. I must tell you that this fellow's attitude towards me has become increasingly intimidating and erratic of late and I am positively in fear of my life.'

Holmes slowly raised his eyes towards the forthright historian and he responded to the man's passion with a wry smile of admiration.

'Very well, Mr Grey, then you shall have it!'

Holmes went over to the mantelpiece and filled up his pipe from the Persian slipper. He drew on it slowly for a moment or two and then laid it back down.

'Now Mr Denbigh Grey, please explain to me exactly how these most singular rendezvous of yours are arranged.'

Holmes smiled encouragingly at the nervous scholar, but there was something else in his manner that implied that he had found a solution to Grey's problem within the last moment or two. The reference to Admiral Nearchus seemed to have set off a chain of thoughts that had negated his previous work upon the blackboard and inspired within him a definitive plan of action. Perhaps his knowledge of ancient history was beyond anything that I had previously thought him capable of?

'These meetings have always been instigated by that odious man with the ginger hair. So far, he has not been negligent enough to either reveal his name to me, or an address whereby he might be reached. A simple card is pushed through my letterbox which states the exact date and time that I should liaise with them in that awful room on Park Street.

'It is there that we make our exchange, I to receive new pages of manuscript and them to accept my completed work. On each occasion, I receive my instructions, as to how much time they will allow for me to complete my work and an oft-repeated warning that I should be both prompt and discreet.

'Recently these warnings have become increasingly intense and I can only assume that they are working within a time limit of their own.' While Grey recalled these arrangements, I could see him become increasingly anxious. Holmes seemed oblivious to this fact and proceeded in the same calm tones that he had previously employed.

'It does seem hard to believe that you have no means of making contact with them of your own instigation. After all, how are they to know if you are unable to meet a deadline, or have a query that you wish to raise with them?'

'Although I am yet to make use of this facility, there is a certain small tobacconist on the corner near my rooms in Holborn. The proprietor has been instructed to receive messages from me and then to pass them on to the two Germanic gentlemen, should I need to contact them urgently. However I am only supposed to do so under the most extreme of circumstances.'

Holmes clapped his hands together, resoundingly and gleefully.

'That is most excellent, for these are undoubtedly extreme circumstances and this arrangement will suit my purposes very well indeed!' he exclaimed.

Again Grey turned to me for an explanation and once again I had to disappoint him.

'I do not understand to what purpose you are referring. You seem to have abandoned every hope that you might have had of breaking the code.' I pointed to the empty blackboard in exasperation.

'I am afraid that once again, Watson, you are guilty of jumping to conclusions far too quickly. It has not even occurred to you that I wiped away my work, not because I had lost any hope of ever breaking the code, but simply because I did not need it anymore.'

'Do you mean to say that you have already broken the code?' Grey asked incredulously.

Holmes could not resist a subtle, self-satisfied smile as he nodded his confirmation.

'You might call it that,' Holmes replied enigmatically.

'Would you care to enlighten us?' I asked sarcastically.

'You know my method, Watson; I still require further data before I will be able to confirm my findings. In the meantime, however, I will send off two wires and I require the full address of the point of rendezvous from you, Mr Grey.'

I handed my notebook to the bemused historian and he scribbled out an address in nearby Park Street. Then Holmes grabbed the book and proceeded to write an extensive list of instructions, which he handed to Denbigh Grey.

'I am sure that your employers are familiar with your hand. So please copy this out, word for word and leave this with your tobacconist without a moment's delay.' With no word of explanation, Holmes dismissed Grey in a most offhand manner and he then summoned Mrs Hudson, to whom he handed the wires for immediate despatch.

'There is nothing more that I will be able to do for a full twenty-four hours,' Holmes announced.

He folded himself into his meditative position on his chair by the fire and without another word he closed his eyes. I realized, having experienced this numerous times before, that this was my cue to find a silent occupation of my own.

I picked up one of the papers and began to read an article on page two that dealt with the Whitechapel ritual killing, but in a far less sensationalist manner than had the original report. Evidently Commissioner Bradford's involvement and influence were already having a meretricious effect.

I delved deeper into the paper, but soon realized that my mind was constantly wandering away from whichever article I had first focussed on. As far as I had been aware, Holmes had been no closer to solving the riddle of Grey's manuscript than he had been at the beginning of his task. Why had this erroneous reference to the death of Nearchus convinced Holmes that he was no longer in need of the earlier clues?

As far as I had been aware, Holmes had no knowledge of or interest in the history of Alexander's military campaigns, so therefore I was certain that his reaction had been triggered by a more subtle nuance than bare historical fact. I was in little doubt that this clue would remain solely and safely in Holmes' custody, until such time as he decided to reveal it to me.

Therefore, my mind took off on another tangent and I realized that the Whitechapel business had obliterated all thoughts of Sophie Sinclair. There was, hopefully recovering slowly in her hospital bed, securely watched over by Scotland Yard's finest and I had barely given her welfare a passing thought. I understood Holmes' reasons for my not attending her bedside, but with regret. I had just replaced my paper and I was in the process of filling my pipe, when a gentle knock on our door and a breathless Mrs Hudson announced the arrival of Menachem Goldman.

I must confess that it was only our landlady's announcement that had caused me to recognize our unexpected but welcome visitor. I was surprised to note that Goldman had dramatically altered his appearance since his previous visit to Baker Street, and that he seemed to be of a most furtive disposition.

All traces of the orthodox Polish rabbi had been removed. The long black coat had been replaced with a smart grey overcoat. The traditional, large black hat was now a trimmed grey felt and Goldman was completely clean shaven, save for a neatly trimmed moustache.

'Well I must say, Goldman, your transformation is a remarkable one!' I exclaimed. 'I should not know you, save for your confirmation that it is you standing before us.'

'Dr Watson, I am gratified to hear you say that, because becoming unrecognizable was my undeniable intention.' Goldman was employing his most clipped and eloquent middle-class London accent and he glanced across at Holmes who was still enwrapped in his lotus position.

Suddenly his eyes sparked back into life, he slapped both arms of his chair and jumped up in a most jovial disposition.

'Well of course it is and I am most gratified to see it!' Holmes cried out. Then, in answer to our confused expressions, he added, 'I am certain that you would only obliterate your former guise if you felt that your ability to function in your murky chosen profession was becoming jeopardized by it.'

'Well I am glad to know that my discomfort is a source of pleasure to you, Mr Holmes!' Goldman's sarcastic response was indicative of his disturbed state of mind.

'You misunderstand me, Goldman, it is

not your state of unease which I find gratifying, it is the cause of it that intrigues me. For me it is only ever the work that matters.'

'On this occasion the work has not only brought about a change in my persona, but it has very nearly cost me both my profession and my life! The lava pit into which you have thrown me is a place from which it is almost impossible to escape. It is only because of my knowledge and the quickness of my wits that I am able to stand before you today.

'This mandolin of yours, Mr Holmes, is the most troublesome object that I have ever become associated with. Nobody is willing to speak of it and the very mention of it has caused a look of fear to cross every face that I have addressed upon the subject.'

'Yet, despite the problematic nature of your inquiries, you have made some progress, I perceive. Watson, he surely would not be here otherwise,' he added for my benefit.

'I am afraid that I have not been able to identify the thief himself, nor do I think that I shall ever be able to. All I can tell you, with any certainty, is that the thief is now no longer in this country and that he was in the employ of a certain Professor Sydney of the British Museum. Therefore, the police theory that it was an inside job has been totally validated.'

'Hah! Well that is about all that Bradstreet and his band of men have been able to achieve so far! However, I believe that you have more to tell me, Goldman, much more,' Holmes invited.

'Indeed I do, Mr Holmes, indeed I do. I have spent much of my time posing as the designated agent for the sale of this damnable mandolin and I have slowly come to realize that the people behind its theft are more powerful and therefore potentially more dangerous than any that I have previously encountered.

'Their organization was not even affected by the untimely death of their principal, Professor Sydney, and their influence crosses many borders. I paid a visit to one of my oldest friends, Jacob Bloomberg of Düsseldorf, and he warned me that certain people had heard of my masquerading as the negotiating agent and that they wanted to ask me a few questions.

'At once, I knew exactly what Jacob meant by that and that a polite conversation was the last thing on their minds! There and then I resolved to lose my beloved rabbi with all speed and I relocated my office without a moment's delay. With renewed confidence I continued my enquiries and piece by piece, I collected what information I could.

'The theft of the mandolin had been financed by a private collector in Bavaria. His name has been whispered in certain corners of the underworld, but I assure you, Mr Holmes, that nobody in their right mind would reveal his name, neither under threat nor persuasion. All I can tell you is that he is securely ensconced within a large, renovated castle that is perched upon a small mountain that overlooks the Austro/ Bavarian border.

'Within the castle, the Neuschwanstein, resides the instigator of your theft and you should be under no illusion, Mr Holmes, that within its walls, he is virtually untouchable. The castle was originally commissioned by King Ludwig II of Bavaria and he helped design it in the idealized fashion of the Romanesque Revival, before he abandoned it due to diminished funds just before his death in 1886.

'More relevantly, Ludwig also designed the building with security very much in mind, for his intention was to live out the remainder of his life as a total and unreachable recluse. The current occupant bought the castle with that same priority and he spent a vast fortune in completing the work and in rendering it as secure as possible. Consequently, he is seldom seen, save for a small group of his confidants, who commute on a regular basis from the castle to Austria and back again.

'The owner remains anonymous and of the few who have been afforded a brief glimpse of the man, all but one has stated that his entire head is swathed in a black silken mask!'

'That is a remarkable if over-elaborate report, Goldman. The reference to a mask is somewhat suggestive as is the location of this reclusive individual. I now have grave doubts that the mandolin can ever be reclaimed.'

I was surprised by Holmes' defeatist attitude, but more so by the somewhat nonchalant manner in which he had received Goldman's hard-won information. It was almost as if he had been expecting to hear this testimony and that Goldman's report had really been nothing more than an irrelevant confirmation. Once again I was left wondering what Holmes had found so significant in the name Nearchus.

Nevertheless, Holmes heartily congratulated Goldman on his discoveries and I noticed that he had pressed a folded compensation into the ready palm of the former rabbi as he led him to the door.

Once the door had been closed behind our much-altered associate, I immediately insisted on an explanation from my friend.

'Despite your assurances that we were going to see this thing through to the end and in tandem, it seems that once again you have chosen to keep me in the dark,' I protested.

'Whatever do you mean?'

'Oh come along Holmes, I know you well enough to have recognized the fact that the majority of Goldman's information came as no surprise to you whatsoever! Even the reference to a black mask seemed to leave you unmoved. Would you mind explaining to me exactly what all of this means?' I insisted.

'Watson, you have heard and seen everything that I have done and the reason for my reticence in revealing more to you is that there really is nothing more that I can add to what you already know. Anything else would be mere speculation on my part and I would not want to further muddy the waters, until the moment that I can confirm my hypothesis.'

This was a statement of intent that Holmes had expounded on far too many occasions in the past. This time I was determined that I simply would not let matters lie. I was about to offer a further protest when I was immediately halted in my tracks by yet another, though less welcome, interruption. A rather apologetic Mrs Hudson announced and then showed into our room two sheepish and crestfallen inspectors from Scotland Yard.

They each apologized in turn for having failed to make any real progress in their respective investigations. Lestrade at least had finally located the constable who had been supplanted by my attacker that afternoon at the Garrick Theatre. His lifeless body had been found, trussed up in a large wicker hamper that had formerly been used to store worn and redundant costumes. The fact that the hamper was seldom used had resulted in the delay in finding the dead policeman.

Bradstreet was no closer to identifying the thief at the museum than he had been at the beginning of his search and both men sank down into their seats as if expecting a rebuke from my friend. Consequently, the three of us were completely thrown off of our guards when Holmes, quite inexplicably, began to laugh uproariously.

'Well I must say, from looking at your

faces, any impartial observer would presume that you had both carried out the crimes yourselves!' he explained, between bursts of merriment.

Both men appeared to have been as relieved as they were bemused.

'Inspectors Bradstreet and Lestrade, you must not be too hard upon yourselves — you really should not. Do not forget that we are not dealing with a group of commonplace or run-of-the-mill criminals. These are a highly organized group of intelligent and determined people with more than one mastermind formulating their schemes, not to mention unlimited resources behind them.

'I assure you both that Miss Sinclair's attacker and the museum thief are one and the same and I am of little doubt that he is now somewhere abroad and well out of our reach. Nevertheless, all is not yet lost, for I have deduced that he is a minor cog within the wheels of a far more complex machine.

'I propose, therefore, that we rendez-vous here, tomorrow evening at six-thirty post meridian when, if you would indulge me with just a little patience and fortitude, I will present you both with a far bigger fish for you to fry!'

Both men nodded their agreement with great enthusiasm, although this diminished somewhat when Holmes also advised them to come bearing arms. Nevertheless, they were both determined to keep this appointment and of course, I offered my own meagre support.

Even at this stage, I was still no closer to understanding the motivation behind Holmes' proposal but I was now resigned to remaining ignorant of the facts until the following evening.

11

The Austrian Spy

The next twenty-four hours passed excruciatingly slowly. However, the anticipation of knowing that something dramatic and conclusive awaited us was not the only factor that rendered the wait so agonizing.

My friend, Sherlock Holmes, was not the most patient of people at the best of times. However, when the scent of blood filled his nostrils, he strained upon his leash with the power of a hundred foxhounds.

Holmes spent much of the remainder of the day in pacing up and down in our room, occasionally punctuating this walking marathon with grunts and snarls of frustration. He exhausted the rest of his time in sitting by the fire, all the while pumping his fingers violently upon the arms of his chair in an irritating rhythm.

Once or twice he had even picked up his violin and bow, but the discordant scratching that he produced soon became too much even for him to bear and the instrument was immediately discarded with disdain.

Consequently, it was with some relief that I noted the lateness of the hour and I was able to make my way up to my room, without appearing to be unsupportive. However, the quest for sleep soon became a thankless and fruitless task for us both and before very long we two found ourselves back in the sitting room once more.

By this time, of course, the fire was quite dead and a dark chill had penetrated our small room. Holmes pulled his purple dressing gown tightly towards him and he thrust his hands into its pockets once he had lit his pipe. With a smile he noticed my look of anticipation, as I stared at him from my chair opposite.

'I suppose that you would like to know the reason behind my mysterious arrangements for tomorrow evening?' he asked with a feigned reluctance.

'Well of course I would!' I confirmed emphatically.

'Very well then.' Holmes pulled long and leisurely upon his pipe before continuing.

'You could not have failed to notice the change that had come over the appearance of Denbigh Grey, when compared to your original impression of the man, I presume?'

'He certainly appeared to be somewhat tired and dissipated and his nerves were undoubtedly stretched to their limits,' I offered.

'I am certain that his observation of Daxer's manner towards him was an understatement in the extreme. We know, from past experience[1], that Daxer is a most indomitable force and the greater urgency that he now seems to attach to Grey's work indicates to me that Daxer himself is coming under extreme pressure to bring the whole business to a rapid conclusion.

'To Daxer, that would be an intolerable situation in which to find himself and I am certain that Grey's life will soon be under a greater threat than ever before!'

'Yet you allowed him to leave here without even an escort or guidance?' I asked in dismay and disbelief.

'Not without guidance, Watson, I assure you. For as long as he is progressing with the work, Daxer will refrain from making a move against him. Grey's services are almost unique and therefore invaluable to Daxer and his people. However, I have now advised him to send an urgent message to Daxer, informing him that he no longer felt able or willing to continue with the work.'

'You have also signed his death warrant at the same time! Grey's life will not be worth a moment's purchase, once Daxer receives that note of yours.' I was aghast as I listened to Holmes' flagrant disregard of our client's wellbeing.

Holmes smiled benignly in response to my protest and shook his head.

'Grey has offered to return the remaining manuscript to Daxer, at their usual meeting place in Park Street tomorrow evening. However, Grey will be otherwise engaged, at his aunt's house in

Camberwell, having dinner. The four of us will be in Park Street in his stead, when the mystery of the Alexandrian manuscript will finally be revealed!'

'Not to mention the capture of a dangerous and elusive international spy into the bargain! I salute you Holmes and apologize for ever having doubted you.'

'You should not be too hasty with your congratulations, Watson. I can promise you that Daxer will not be alone in Park Street tomorrow evening and there is still much work to be done and danger to negotiate before we can start slapping each other on the back.'

Holmes' brief explanation had done much to calm my bewildered frame of mind. Consequently, within a few minutes I found myself ready for my bed once more. I left Holmes where I had found him and he assured me with a smile and a nod that he would be fine.

Before finally retiring, I brought out my trusty army revolver from its locked drawer and I gave it a brief, albeit superfluous examination. Holmes had left me in little doubt that in a few hours' time its services would be called upon once more.

In view of the challenge that now lay before us, I was somewhat surprised to find that my friend was in a most disturbed and distressed frame of mind when I went down for breakfast the following morning.

I thought it best that I should maintain my silence for a while, but a brief look at Holmes told me that he had not made use of his bed the night before. His gown was still tightly drawn in, his hair was in disarray and his eyes were dark and bloodshot. Then I observed the obvious cause of his disturbance; a short wire that lay on the floor by his feet.

I asked him if I might glance at its contents and he agreed, albeit somewhat indifferently. I was rather perplexed once I realized that the wire had nothing whatsoever to do with any of our current cases. Rather, it referred to one of our previous investigations, namely the murder of Christophe Decaux.

The wire had been sent by Inspector Gregson of recent dubious repute and he stated briefly and in extreme confidence that the premature release of Decaux's murderer, Roger Ashley, had come to his attention within the last few hours. The justification for Ashley's early release and its instigator were unknown to him, but the grounds for the successful appeal had been that the original evidence had been ruled as circumstantial on a second and closer examination.

'Why, this is disgraceful and utter nonsense!' I exclaimed. 'Lestrade and the two of us managed to build a completely watertight case that could not be shaken, even by the wiles and ploys of the late Austin-Simons. Who could be responsible for this utter travesty?'

Then another thought also occurred to me.

'Why would this note have come from Gregson and not Lestrade? After all, it was Lestrade who had initiated the original prosecution and Gregson had no involvement in that business at all!'

My second barrage of questions finally managed to rouse Holmes from his listless and lethargic reaction to this act of treachery. He pushed his hair back from his eyes as he pulled a cigarette from the pocket of his dressing gown.

'Watson, it is somewhat easier for me to answer your second list of questions than your first. I would say with confidence that Lestrade could not possibly have sent us the wire, for the simple reason that he was not actually made aware of Ashley's release! Whoever did instigate his pardon would surely have made certain that Lestrade was kept in the dark, if for no other reason than to ensure that we remained unaware of it also.

'If Gregson ever felt any allegiance to the brotherhood before the incident in Whitechapel, that would surely have dissipated from the instant that he incurred the gunshot wound at their hands. Prior to his strange behaviour at Pike's club, Gregson's record had always been unquestionable if uninspiring and I feel sure that he must have been placed in a position that seemed torturous to him at the time before he would ever consider neglecting his duties in such a fashion. This wire is surely his way of making amends for his misdemeanour.'

'Now I understand, but who could, or would have brought Ashley's release about? Perhaps more crucially, what could have been the motive for such a miscarriage of justice?'

By now my questioning and his responses had gone some way towards alleviating Holmes' malaise. My last question, however, brought about another alteration to his disposition. A pained expression, such as I had seldom seen before, contorted his face as he grappled with a seemingly unfathomable dilemma. For the first time in many hours, he gave up his seat and then walked over to the windows.

Holmes pulled back the drapes in a surprisingly furtive and cautious manner and he began to stare intently through the glass, as if the answers lay outside on the bustling thoroughfare. He remained frozen in this position for so long that I began to wonder if my request for an answer had been forgotten.

'Watson, there are so many people out there, going about their various tasks and errands, each one of them unaware of the fact that there is a clandestine agency observing and controlling their every action and even their entire way of life! Only we few have a vague understanding of the power and influence that they wield and are therefore able to put up a spirited, if inadequate form of resistance. Nevertheless, I would be loath to admit that the actions of so vast a population are being reduced to utter futility by so few.'

He turned towards me bearing a pained smile.

'Yet perhaps there is still a chance that we might be able to put matters to rights.' Holmes' attempt at assurance lacked any great conviction, but I was determined to grab hold of even that faint hope.

'Well of course there is! Perhaps the events of the coming evening might go some way to accomplishing that?' I proposed, with as much enthusiasm as I could muster. 'However, you have not yet answered my other questions,' I insisted.

'The motive for Ashley's liberation is highly questionable and as you know full well, I will never succumb to such idle speculation. As to whom, well, I will only say that there is but one man in this country who is able to exert such power and influence.' In anticipation of my next question, Holmes held up his hand to ward off another word upon the subject and I knew that nothing I could have said would draw him out any further, for now.

We spent much of the remainder of the day by the fire, Holmes with his pipes and I with the daily papers. Inevitably, Holmes refused all of Mrs Hudson's attempts at getting him to take some food and I ended up taking both a lonely luncheon and supper.

As the day drew on, we both noticed that a grey thick mist had slowly been rising from the chilled, damp ground. Consequently, by nightfall a thick, all-consuming and treacherous fog had enwrapped the streets outside. It seemed to be somehow appropriate that our undertaking was to be shrouded in these conditions, although our task would now be made all the more problematical by the muffling effect of the fog upon our adversary's approach.

At the appointed hour, Lestrade and Bradstreet walked uncertainly into our rooms. We were all dressed for a long, cold night's work and the two policemen immediately warmed themselves by our blazing fire.

'I trust that I have not been lured away from my own fire by some wild goose chase of yours, Mr Holmes.'

Lestrade was his usual surly self and he chided Holmes almost as soon as he felt warm enough to turn briefly away from the flames. By the time of their arrival, Holmes had resurrected himself from the dark chasm into which he had earlier descended. He had put his toilet to right and he was rubbing his hands together both in anticipation and in an attempt to generate extra warmth. He was in his heaviest coat and his favourite muffler.

'Well, Inspector Lestrade, that would very much depend on whether you consider Herr Theodore Daxer to be a migratory bird of some kind!'

'Oh really Mr Holmes, so you are about to present us with the notorious

Austrian spy, are you?' At the very mention of Daxer's name, both policemen seemed to recoil from the enormity of the task that lay ahead, despite the obvious benefits to their careers that Daxer's apprehension might present.

Obviously it was the latter consideration that weighed most heavily with them both and they then checked their firearms and handcuffs with renewed care and enthusiasm.

'Should we not be going now, Mr Holmes?' Bradstreet asked.

'There is still one member of our party yet to arrive, namely London's finest cabby, Gunner King,' Holmes announced.

'Surely the distance to Park Street is eminently walkable?' I suggested.

'You are forgetting, Watson, that King is also a most stalwart ally of ours and it will be his task this evening to ensure that our quarry do not leave prematurely by the rear exit!' Holmes explained emphatically.

Our wait was only to be a short one, for a moment or two later we could hear

King's vehicle pull up outside 221b. The ominous fog had not inhibited King's rapid progress to Park Street, for it was a journey that he could well have completed while blindfolded! We jumped out from the cab in plenty of time and King promptly made his way to the rear of the building to begin his vigil.

Number seventy-four was unique from the remainder of the smart town houses that adorned that section of the road, for it was the only building that was so woefully and badly maintained. Most of the paintwork had either peeled away or fallen off altogether and the brickwork and pointing were in a sorry state of disrepair.

As predicted by Denbigh Grey, the street door latch was hanging on by the merest thread and we made our way up to the first floor uninhibited. Following Grey's instructions, we crept along a damp and musty corridor that led to a large open room, which would, no doubt, have been the sitting room, at some point in its sorry history.

There was something infectious about

those dismal surroundings and we each searched for a hiding place with a sense of foreboding. We found it difficult to conceal ourselves in a room so bereft of furnishings, although I found a place behind a large wing-backed chair that had lost the majority of its upholstery.

Bradstreet and Lestrade assumed their positions on either side of the door, while Holmes sat himself upon my chair, wearing a bowler hat similar to the type that Grey often wore. Holmes had given us full instructions and he held his lamp, poised to lift the flap at a moment's notice.

We had arrived well ahead of Grey's appointed time and consequently it became a long, tense wait. We decided to refrain from smoking throughout, lest any smoke might drift down the stairs and alert our Austrian visitors and we were all well able to maintain an absolute silence.

The room was swathed in complete darkness. There were no gas or oil lights, so at least we were assured of the effectiveness of Holmes' lamp. The swirling fog obscured much of the light from the street lamps and so it took us some time to adjust our eyes to this all-pervading gloom. Slowly, however, we became able to pick each other out, merely by being able to recognize each other's shadows and I saw Lestrade and Bradstreet remove their firearms as the time for Daxer's arrival drew ever closer.

All the while Holmes maintained the stillness of a statue. His back remained straight and erect and his hand did not leave the flap to his lamp, even once. I sensed the same tension in the others when we heard the sound of a vehicle pull up outside. However, Holmes immediately checked his pocket watch and assured us, in the most hushed of whispers that the sound had been caused by King assuming his position at the rear of the building.

A barely audible exhalation of breath heralded a few moments of relaxation. However, that was not destined to last for very long. The silent street outside had been further insulated by the thickening fog. Consequently, the Austrian's vehicle had arrived without having made either a sign or sound. This phenomenon very nearly caught us off guard, for the first that we knew of Daxer's arrival had been the sound of the front door being pushed open against the exterior wall.

The fact that the Austrians were expecting to meet Grey there and not ourselves obviously worked to our advantage. As a consequence, their approach was far less cautious than it might otherwise have been. We could clearly make out the sound of two men climbing the stairs. Their footsteps were heavy and there was a clear delay between the sound of one set of boots and the other.

We all cocked our guns before the footsteps reached the landing on our floor, for it was almost impossible to do so in total silence. I was the only one of our group to have the advantage of being able to witness the approach of the two spies. However, the man coming towards us was unknown to me.

I was horrified to note that he hesitated a long time before deciding whether to enter the room or not. I could not tell whether or not he was waiting for his comrade to arrive. Perhaps something had aroused his suspicion and our trap had been sprung? Whatever the reason, he remained on the landing and I was therefore able to take note of his appearance.

He was considerably taller than his colleague, although much slimmer of build. He was no less forbidding in appearance nonetheless. He was dressed entirely in black, he had a set of broad and aggressive shoulders and his fearsome face was adorned with a huge, unkempt black moustache and a terrible scar than ran from the side of his left eye down to the top edge of his lips.

'Mr Grey?' he called out in a hoarse Germanic voice.

The ensuing silence evidently made him all the more suspicious and he still made no indication that he was ready to enter the room.

'Why will you not reveal yourself? You have nothing to fear. We merely wish to retrieve our property.'

At that moment a familiar shape appeared at the scarred man's shoulder. It was a sight that sent a shiver of dread and revulsion running through me.

The two men moved slowly forward and now, of course, they could see the shape of the hat that Holmes had upon his head. This time it was Daxer's voice that echoed around the dilapidated room.

'Mr Grey, I am rapidly running out of patience! Reveal yourself now or I assure you that it will be all the worse for you when you finally do!'

Holmes held his nerve and remained still and silent until the two spies had finally crossed the threshold into the room.

'Mr Grey!! This is your final warning!' Daxer screamed hysterically.

By now Daxer and his colleague, who we were later able to identify as being the assassin Carl Irving, were clear of the door. Without warning Lestrade stepped forward and slammed the door shut behind them! The Austrians were so stunned by this action that they had not even been aware of the presence of Bradstreet immediately next to them.

The two policemen pressed their

revolvers into the temples of the two spies, while at the same time Holmes and I finally rose to our feet to face them. Holmes opened up the flap to his lamp and shone it directly into the eyes of Theodore Daxer!

'Good evening, Herr Daxer. It was very good of you to keep our appointment.' Holmes smiled a sardonic greeting.

'Where is Denbigh Grey?' Daxer asked, although he seemed to sense that it was a futile question and that the historian was already well out of harm's way.

'I can assure you, Herr Daxer, that he is currently enjoying a most pleasant evening and that he is now completely out of your reach.'

'I should have known. A man like Grey was not capable of writing such a note to me. He did not have the nerve to defy me! You have worked this thing very well, Mr Holmes, I congratulate you.'

Holmes bowed in acknowledgement and then signalled that Bradstreet and Lestrade should now apply their hand-cuffs. To encourage the spies' compliance, I levelled my own revolver at them and the inspectors lowered theirs at the same time.

'For what crime are we to be arrested?' Daxer asked calmly. 'I know of no law that prevents the translation of an ancient manuscript. We have done nothing more than that.'

Unfortunately, for all concerned, Irving's nerve did not hold up as well as that of his associate. Before Holmes even had a chance to answer Daxer, much less to ask him some vital questions of his own, Irving threw off Lestrade's attempts at restraining him and managed to avoid having the handcuffs closed upon his wrists.

Then, with a display of agility and strength that belied his appearance, Irving threw the inspector halfway across the room. Lestrade was sent crashing into the far wall and with such a force that he remained still and unconscious upon the floor.

Irving was now free to bring his gun into play and Holmes only narrowly avoided one of his bullets by flinging himself to the floor, behind the large chair that he had been seated upon just a moment before.

My first instinct was to see if Lestrade needed my immediate consideration. However, my attention was soon diverted by the sight of Irving levelling his revolver in the direction of Inspector Bradstreet. In an instant I remembered Holmes' reaction after I had prematurely ended the life of Austin-Simons, thereby depriving Holmes of the secrets that had died with him.

Consequently my aim was adjusted to Carl Irving's leg and I fired with the intention of only disabling the Austrian. Irving's gun immediately fell onto the threadbare rug as he frantically clutched at his thigh. His cry of pain echoed around the large, dark, empty room and he fell to the floor as the blood pumped out onto his desperate hands. Now Bradstreet turned his attention to Daxer and soon the two burly men were engaged in a titanic struggle for the control of Daxer's gun.

Despite Bradstreet's noble efforts, Daxer proved to be indomitable and a blow upon Bradstreet's head from Daxer's gun handle left the detective sprawled out upon the floor. Daxer and I now faced each other, with our weapons trained upon the other. I could tell from the flash of menace in Daxer's demonic eyes that he was as determined as I to see this scenario through to its conclusion.

Neither of us would waver nor flinch. Our guns stayed level and still and we both remained steadfast in our intentions. Then, to my dismay, Daxer suddenly switched his aim. His gun was now bearing down upon the motionless head of Inspector Bradstreet.

'Do not look so surprised, Dr Watson, when have you ever known me to play by the rules? I assure you that should you not drop your weapon immediately and kick it over towards me, I will shoot out your friend's eyes in an instant! I think you already know that I will carry out my threat should you not.'

Even in the darkened room I could see Daxer's malicious grin as he pulled back the trigger. I had little choice other than to comply with his demands. Even if I had managed to shoot first, there was little doubt that Daxer would still have been able to fire at Bradstreet before he fell. After all, he was standing at point blank range. Besides, Holmes still remained out of sight and I could not be sure as to his intentions.

That fact had not gone unnoticed, and as soon as Daxer had retrieved my revolver from the floor, he turned his attention towards my friend. With his gun aimed at my head, Daxer demanded that Holmes should show himself without delay.

'As you know, Mr Holmes, I am more than capable of shooting the good doctor in cold blood. Besides, we have much to talk about, you and I.' Only Theodore Daxer could make an invitation to talk sound like a sentence of death.

'Indeed we have Herr Daxer.' Holmes slowly stood up and Daxer immediately indicated that Holmes should place his hands upon the top of his head.

As can be imagined, I was much relieved to see that Holmes had decided to comply with the Austrian spy's demands, but I was also much confused by Holmes' bravado in the face of defeat.

'What were you thinking of, Mr Holmes, when you devised this elaborate scheme to entrap me? Had my nervous friend not, as you English say, upturned your apple cart, I am certain that you would have succeeded in doing so. But to what gain? I am certain that you only sent me that note because you had already broken the code. Yet you could surely not have been so arrogant as to assume that I was not as capable of breaking the code as you were?'

'Had you done so, I am sure that I would not still be standing here and having this conversation now,' Holmes stated simply, but I could sense that Holmes was stalling for time. My hopes were raised further when the corner of my eye caught sight of Lestrade slowly and silently slithering towards his own gun.

'You will tell me precisely what you have discovered, or your friend here will surely face the dire consequences of your defiance.' Holmes' assumption had been an accurate one and it had clearly struck a nerve with Daxer, who now seemed more determined than ever to put a bullet through my brain.

Daxer moved within a couple of feet of me and therefore Lestrade's painful progress was now behind his field of vision. Holmes was also aware of this fact, for he continued to protract his conversation with Daxer.

'Perhaps you could satisfy my own curiosity by explaining to me what you intend to do with this information, once you have it. After all, you fully intend to kill us both in either event, so to confide in me now would not cause you too much of an inconvenience.'

'It is a pity, Mr Holmes that even now you do not realize that, for once, we were playing on the same side! My loyalties are and always have been to the noble house of Hapsburg and the Austro-Hungarian Empire. The Bavarian Brotherhood and their vast array of associates are as much an enemy of ours as they are of you and your government.' Daxer shook his head despondently, but he failed to notice that, for once, Holmes had been as perplexed by Daxer's amazing revelation as I had been.

He had also been unaware that Lestrade had finally managed to reclaim his weapon and that it was aimed straight at Daxer! The Austrian was momentarily distracted by the sound of Lestrade pulling back his trigger and this gave me the opportunity that I needed.

Daxer's close proximity to me allowed me to grab his gun hand and I managed to twist it round, almost to breaking point. The gun crashed to the floor and Holmes leapt from his chair and on to it in a single movement. Daxer seemed to realize that there was still much for us to learn from him and that Holmes and I would only shoot him as a very last resort.

Therefore, instead of raising his hands in surrender, Daxer shoved me directly into Holmes' path as he made a dash for the door! Holmes directed me to attend to the injured men and he then tore off after Daxer without a second's delay.

For a moment or two, I was torn between my Hippocratic Oath and my duty to my friend. However, I was also in the certain knowledge that Holmes was armed and that Theodore Daxer clearly was not. So I decided to turn my attention towards the three injured parties that littered the room around me.

Lestrade was slowly recovering from his collision with the wall and Bradstreet was rousing himself from his own state of unconsciousness. Therefore I realized that my priority was undoubtedly Carl Irving.

I had taken great pains to ensure that my shot would not have proved to be a fatal one and I had therefore aimed at his leg. Consequently, my dismay upon discovering that my bullet had actually penetrated Irving's femoral artery can be well understood. That particular vessel expels blood at an alarming rate and consequently, unless attended to within seconds of penetration, the amount of blood loss usually leads to an almost immediate fatality. To my consternation, this had proved to be the case with Carl Irving.

Consequently, I could only console myself with the thought that Holmes might have been able to extract enough information from Daxer to deflect his ire away from my perceived carelessness. In truth, I felt that I had done well in hitting Irving's leg under the dramatic circumstances that were all around me, but I could not be certain that Holmes would have seen it that way.

Therefore, I left Bradstreet and Lestrade to their own devices and once I was certain that Irving had breathed his last, I reclaimed my revolver and followed Holmes down the stairs with all speed. As I reached the landing, I was taken aback by the sound of a terrible commotion that emanated from the street below.

I was relieved that there been no sound of gunfire, but there had clearly been an almighty crash and the high-pitched squeal of several frightened horses was inescapable. I was greeted on reaching street level by the horrific sight of the mangled form of Theodore Daxer lying crushed and broken beneath the rear wheel of an onrushing horse-drawn omnibus!

Daxer's body was splayed out at an unusual, distorted angle, which made it look as if every bone in his rib cage had been crushed by the thundering horses' hooves and the large wheels of the omnibus. His clothes had been splattered profusely with an unsightly mixture of horses' excretion, mud and his own blood. His face had been similarly treated and his twisted mouth was oozing an unusually dark stream of blood from each corner.

Miraculously, however, the damnable man was still clinging onto the last painful remnants of his life. He even seemed to be anxious to communicate with Holmes, who had bent down to catch the last words that the Austrian spy would ever utter. I moved closer myself, so that I could note every word.

Daxer's final, rasping words were as malevolent as one would have expected from him. However, as brief and inscrutable as they undoubtedly were, they had an effect on Holmes that was sudden and profound. Daxer twisted his evil lips into a contorted smile for one last time.

'You are a bigger fool than even I thought you to be, Mr Holmes. Even now, you still do not realize that I, oh yes I Theodore Daxer, was your brother Mycroft's only hope. I will surely spit upon you both from the very gates of hell!' Daxer even managed a final horrific laugh that caused the blood to seep through his disgusting teeth, before his life was finally extinguished.

Holmes and I slowly stood up and made our way up the stairs to consult with the two inspectors, both of whom appeared to be none the worse for wear. They dashed away to organize the removal of all traces of the scene of carnage on the street below. Obviously, Gunner King had not been oblivious to the sounds of commotion and he pulled up outside the house within a few moments of the collision.

However, it was Holmes' manner and countenance that troubled me the most. Daxer's words had clearly bothered him greatly and he considered Daxer's warning to be a threat to his brother's life that was to be taken with all seriousness. We journeyed back to Baker Street in silence and Holmes would not be drawn upon the subject of his brother, until we were back in our rooms and into our pipes.

Even then, Holmes seemed reluctant to elaborate on his thoughts. As a matter of fact, he appeared to have been as confused as I had been by Daxer's final words, although, of course, they had affected him far more deeply.

Mycroft's position at the Diogenes Club had become more than untenable since the revelations regarding some of his fellow members had cast so many dispersions upon the club's integrity.

'There is little or no action than I can take tonight. I very much doubt that Mycroft will ever again be found at the Diogenes Club, but I will be the first visitor to his office in the morning, I can assure you!' Holmes stated with determination.

Nonetheless, I detected disquiet in his voice and an apprehension in his manner that I found disconcerting in the extreme.

12

The Absent Detective

In view of his current traumatized state of mind, I had been somewhat surprised when Holmes suddenly declared himself ready to retire to his room for the night.

All too often, in circumstances such as these, Holmes was prone to spending the entire night in his chair, usually in a state of meditation and more often than not accompanied by a liberal intake of his old shag tobacco. Consequently, in view of the more personal nature of the current predicament, his decision was even more out of character.

I decided to pour myself out a small glass of port and I smoked a final pipe before making my way up to my own room. However, as I was making my final preparations for bed, a possible and rather disturbing explanation occurred to me.

I made my way gingerly down the stairs once more and opened the top drawer to the desk. I was relieved to see that the leather Moroccan case, which contained Holmes' insidious syringe, was still in its place. Furthermore, by employing Holmes' own method, I was able to deduce from the layer of dust that lay upon the lid of the box that his device had not been put to use in some considerable time.

In a somewhat calmer state of mind, I spent a most restful night and the depth of my sleep had even caused me to come down to breakfast long after my friend had concluded his. It was pleasing to note Holmes' amusement at my hurried and awkward entrance and he was undoubtedly more confident now of finding his brother safe and well and behind his desk in Whitehall.

'So, Watson, I see that your late glass of port had the effect of allaying your customary insatiable appetite!'

In answer to my puzzled expression, Holmes pointed to the tiny traces of the drink that still remained in the bottom of the glass that I had left behind upon the side table.

'By the way, Doctor, should you ever wish to discover whether I have returned to my nasty little indulgence once more, you merely have to ask me. Your habit of leaving the key in an upright position, so that you can tell whether I have used it or not, has surely backfired on you on this occasion.' He laughed.

'As usual, there is very little that seems to escape you!' I replied with a feigned annoyance, as I took my seat at the dining table.

Holmes viewed me with some amusement, while I made very short work of a delicious kipper. He lit a cigarette and leaned back in his chair until my meal was concluded.

'Holmes, I must say that, upon considering the dramatic nature of the events of last night, you appear to be unusually relaxed this morning,' I observed while pushing my plate aside with satisfaction.

'Of course the conclusion of the proceedings was not entirely to my satisfaction and the untimely deaths of both Carl Irving and Theodore Daxer are decidedly inconvenient. Their evidence might well have saved me from a considerable amount of extra work. Nevertheless, I take solace from the fact that matters might very well have culminated in a far more tragic fashion.' Holmes' offhand response belied the anguished manner in which he had received Daxer's dying words.

'Oh come along, Holmes, last night I could tell how Daxer's veiled threat to your brother's wellbeing had affected you. You even proposed an early visit to his offices this morning, presumably to satisfy your own peace of mind. Yet here we both are and you have still not yet galvanized yourself for a visit to Pall Mall. Perhaps an event occurred last night which I have not as yet been made aware of?' I persisted.

'No, not at all, my old friend, but after due consideration, I have been able to adopt an entirely different perspective on the matter. A man of Daxer's vindictive nature will always use his moment of death as a means for exacting his final and irreversible revenge. I would expect nothing more nor less from such a person.

'Nevertheless, I am equally confident that if there were any man in the country who could be deemed as being immune from the iniquitous schemes of the brotherhood, that man would be my brother Mycroft.'

Holmes' confidence in his brother's impregnability was not hard for me to understand. On more than one occasion, most notably during our investigation into the missing Bruce Partington plans, Holmes had referred to Mycroft's unique position in British government. Indeed, in more than one aspect, he could be described as actually being the British government!

There was not a decision made either in the House, or even at Cabinet level, that did not pass through Mycroft's office for scrutiny, analysis and approval. More often than not, his word would be acted upon without a moment's hesitation and there was not a department that did not

317

use his office as an exchange house for information.

Furthermore, Mycroft possessed the same amazing faculties for observation and deduction with which my friend was endowed, although in a slightly more refined and defined form. Unfortunately, he was also the most lethargic and habitual man in London.

A person would be able to set their watch by Mycroft's daily routine. It followed a regular circular course that ran from his rooms in Pall Mall, his offices in Whitehall and hence on to the Diogenes Club. Consequently, Holmes could be reasonably confident of knowing Mycroft's whereabouts at any given time of day.

Therefore, it came as no great surprise to me when Holmes glanced at his watch and announced that now would be a very good time for us to pay Mycroft a visit at his office.

'I am certain that by now he would have received the news of Daxer's death and any insights that he might be able to give us as to its potential repercussions may prove to be invaluable.'

'He may also be able to explain to us the meaning behind Daxer's final words,' I suggested.

'Quite so, quite so,' Holmes agreed as he went to grab his coat.

We arrived at Mycroft's office at the time when the tea lady would normally be bringing her eleven o'clock trolley around. Holmes had been recognized at once by the doorman and we marched directly through to Mycroft's inner sanctum, without delay nor hindrance.

I noticed at once the painting of the owl that hung upon one of his walls and I remembered with embarrassment how that strange depiction had made me suspect Mycroft of having been the elusive third member of the unholy trinity! I also recalled, just as vividly, Holmes' amusement when I decided to voice those same suspicions. My recollections, however, were soon dispelled once we realized that Mycroft's office was conspicuously unoccupied.

Holmes questioned Mycroft's clerk, who we found within his miniscule outer office, the doorman, several officials and even the tea lady! All, however, gave us the same negative response. Mycroft had not been seen at his desk for the last three days. This occurrence was inconceivable to Holmes and the look of angst that I had observed on his face the night before suddenly returned.

We returned to our cab with a good deal more urgency than when we had arrived at Whitehall and Holmes issued his instructions to the driver with a loud, sharp order. Holmes' frustration with the mid morning traffic was excruciatingly obvious and I heard him curse under his breath at every unfortunate delay.

When we arrived at Mycroft's building, Holmes told me to remain in the cab and he dashed up the stairs while leaving the hapless concierge floundering in his wake. Holmes returned to the cab as crestfallen and distraught as he had been before and his last instruction to the driver was to take us to the Diogenes Club in the shortest possible time.

It was hard to stare up at that strikingly austere building without being reminded of the notorious members that it had only recently harboured. Mycroft's association with such a disgraced establishment must have been almost impossible for him to bear. Consequently, when Holmes finally withdrew from his search, I was not in the least bit surprised to observe that his quest there had proved to be as fruitless as the others had been.

Holmes was now so deflated that he could barely summon up the energy to call our address up to the driver. His chin dropped to his chest, he lowered his hat and pulled up his coat collar in an effort at hiding away from his traumatic discoveries. He had now reached the indisputable conclusion that his brother Mycroft had mysteriously disappeared without trace.

'I am certain that there must be a logical explanation for this most singular occurrence,' I ventured, by way of consolation. However, Sherlock Holmes was not to be so easily placated.

He slowly raised his head and shook his head disconsolately.

'In thirty years or more, my brother has

not once deviated from any aspect of his daily routine. The idea of him not going to his office, even for a single day, would be inconceivable to him. He was convinced that were he not in attendance at Whitehall, even for but a few hours, any number of disasters might befall this country. He would not even be a bit surprised if a war should break out during any protracted absence!

'No Watson, I am afraid that something untoward has befallen Mycroft, something that Daxer had apparently been privy to prior to his demise. The only glimmer of hope might lie in something that I learned from his building's concierge.

'The last time that he saw my brother was three mornings ago, at a time when he would normally have been leaving for work. However, Mycroft had made one deviation from his usual routine, for on this occasion he dismissed the use of his customary carriage and instead asked the concierge to summon him a cab. We must find that cab without a moment's delay!'

This realization succeeded in galvanizing Holmes into action and he rapped upon the inside of the cab's roof with the handle of his cane, in an attempt at speeding up our progress. Upon our arrival at Baker Street, Holmes brushed aside the welcome of Mrs Hudson and he dashed up the stairs, leaving his coat and cane strewn in his wake.

By the time that I had gathered up his belongings and made my own more sedate ascent of the stairs, Holmes was already seated at the desk and scrawling hurriedly upon numerous sheets of paper. Once his work had been completed he called down for Mrs Hudson in the most urgent of tones.

The much-harried woman made no secret of her aversion to such treatment and entered our room in an exaggerated nonchalant manner.

'Well I suppose I should be grateful that you are, at least, acknowledging my existence,' she said while crossing her arms in a display of defiance.

Holmes responded with his most charming of smiles and walked over to our landlady with his head bowed suppliantly.

'Mrs Hudson, please accept my most humble apologies for my earlier brutish behaviour. Would you now be so kind as to ensure that the butcher's boy despatches these wires in the shortest possible time? This further note is for the eyes of Gunner King alone. The matter is, I assure you, of the utmost moment.' Holmes smiled.

'Well in that case, I shall see what I can do, Mr Holmes,' she said, while grudgingly taking the papers from him.

'Thank you Mrs Hudson, now go!' Holmes waved her to the door with the back of his hand.

Holmes lit a cigarette and collapsed into his chair as if the effort of writing those notes had exhausted him. However, I was certain that he had, in all probability, been drained by the near certain knowledge that his brother was now in the gravest danger.

Speculation as to the nature and cause of that danger would have been a fruitless exercise in the absence of further data and I was certain that Holmes had also reached that conclusion.

'I can certainly understand the urgency that you have attached to the delivery of the note to King and to its contents. However, I am at a loss as to the proposed recipients of the other two,' I admitted.

'They are intended for my associates and colleagues in Bavaria,' Holmes replied simply. Then, in anticipation of my next question, he added, 'Yes Watson, they are the very correspondents whose wires you so deviously saved from the fire, the contents of which sent you spiralling down a slope towards the most peculiar and erroneous of conclusions!

'I shall say nothing more upon the matter until I have received at least two responses to my wires,' Holmes announced dismissively and I retreated to my chair with a batch of the daily papers.

As the day wore on, I became convinced that Holmes fully intended to be as good as his word. That is not to say that we sat there in total silence for all of that time. Far from it, in fact. For Holmes decided to divert his thoughts away from the fate of his brother, by waxing lyrical upon subjects as diverse as the violin concerto of Bruch and the merits of Dutch cigars over their Cuban counter-parts.

As illuminating as his arguments undoubtedly were, I was becoming increasingly concerned that beneath the surface of his dissertations lurked an underground torrent of dark and forbidding thoughts. I was on the point of inviting him to disclose these to me, when a note arrived from Inspector Lestrade informing us that he was now fully recovered from the traumatic events in Park Street.

He went on to say that Sophie Sinclair had also now returned to full health and that the hospital was discharging her to return home. I was also pleased to note that Lestrade had instructed a local constable to keep a close scrutiny on Miss Sinclair's building. A close scrutiny, but not a constant one, for that would have been too much to expect.

I passed the note over to Holmes who

smiled when he observed the look of concern on my face.

'Well Watson, as I have frequently pointed out, the fairer sex is very much your area of expertise. Consequently I think that a visit to West Hampstead might be a most prudent course of action for you to take.'

'Will you not join me? After all, you might be able to advise her on the best ways of ensuring her security,' I suggested, although without too much enthusiasm.

'No, no, no, it is best that I remain here to await the arrival of my replies. Do not concern yourself, for I shall know where to find you should I need to call upon your services,' Holmes assured me.

Then I became suspicious of Holmes' true motives.

'Will you then confirm that you are not attempting to be rid of me?'

'My dear fellow, I made that very mistake once before, a misjudgement that brought me to within an inch of losing my life! I shall not err in that fashion ever again. Now attend to Miss Sinclair without delay.' Holmes was still smiling, for I could not deceive him as to the true motive for my visit.

I collected my hat and coat without further need of persuasion, but as I turned towards my friend once more, I could see that he had immediately reverted to his dark and introspective disposition. I closed the door behind me with a pang of apprehension that would not be dispelled.

I hurried through a throng of jostling commuters and a brief, icy shower of sleet, before I once more found myself aboard a train bound for West Hampstead. By the time that I had reached my destination the shower had dispersed and the clearing skies revealed a shimmering half moon and the early stages of a savage frost.

I was most mindful of my footing as I neared Miss Sinclair's address, but then another thought stopped me in my tracks. Had the chemistry between us that had seemed so obvious to me at the time of our first meeting been recognized by her as well? Would my visit to her rooms be greeted with the same enthusiasm that had compelled me to go there in the first place?

I lit a cigarette and retraced my paces until I was certain that I could not have been seen from her window. As I stood there, confused by my own uncertainty, I began to feel rather foolish. In the face of all that Miss Sinclair had endured, my present predicament suddenly paled into insignificance and I completed the short walk to her door with determination.

As she slowly opened the door to me, one brief and awkward glance at her pale, drawn face brought home to me the traumas and pain that she had endured as a result of that ghastly attack. She smiled tearfully as soon as she recognized me and I knew at once that my feelings for her were undoubtedly reciprocated.

Her soft, slight hand slipped effortlessly into mine and she led me gently through the front door before she closed it softly behind us. I gratefully accepted her offer of a cup of tea, but while she was preparing the pot, I noticed with horror a packed trunk and several smaller items of luggage stacked up together next to the far wall.

'I see that you are making preparations for a long journey,' I observed tremulously.

She glanced across at her own luggage, as if she had forgotten that it was even there.

'I know that Inspector Lestrade has most kindly provided me with the services of a local constable, but I am equally certain that he will not be able to keep an eye on me all the time. I fully understand that the people who wish to silence me are as ruthless as they are determined. Therefore, I have decided to leave London until the good inspector is certain that the threat to my life has been removed.' Miss Sinclair explained herself calmly and succinctly, but I also detected a hint of regret in her voice that I selfishly welcomed.

At this point I debated with myself as to whether I should broach the subject of the tragic Adele Fox. Had Miss Sinclair already been informed of the death of her friend? Would it have been insensitive of me to mention it if she had not, or would it have been immoral of me not to? After all, they had been the closest of friends. In the end I decided that she had already suffered more than most women could bear and that her continued ignorance would be no bad thing.

'I understand entirely, but where will you go?' I asked with a feigned detachment.

'My Aunt Lydia has a smallholding near the village of Frinton, on the Essex coast. She has been quite alone since the death of my Uncle Cuthbert seven years ago and she has since become rather frail. It will be an arrangement of equal benefit and an opportunity for me to reacquaint myself with my closest living relative.'

'Of course, but be assured that Holmes and I will be working tirelessly, in order to bring about the downfall of those that threaten you,' I assured her with determination.

She smiled serenely and although she bore all the signs of a convalescent, the warm glow that shone from her eyes whenever she smiled reminded me that my journey there had certainly not been made in vain.

'In that case I am sure that I will not be away for too long,' she replied. 'Besides, all of the best stage work is to be found in London, so I simply cannot afford to delay my return. My cousin Wilfred will be on his way home from India in but a few weeks, so I shall have no qualms about deserting my aunt once he arrives.'

'In the meantime, of course, we can correspond regularly, if you are willing,' I proposed.

'Yes, I should like that.' By now the tea had turned quite cold and Miss Sinclair abandoned the cups to her sink, untouched. I noticed her glance rather anxiously at her clock.

'At what time do you intend to depart?'

'I am afraid to say that Tommy will be arriving with his horse and trap in but a few minutes.'

'Who, may I ask, is Tommy?' Although my tone was jocular, I sincerely hoped that I had succeeded in disguising a pang of jealousy from my question that did me no credit.

Evidently I had failed in that, for she laughed as she gave her reply.

'Oh my dear Dr Watson, Tommy is a young delivery boy who works for the local hardware store and he has agreed to take me and my luggage to the station. You may wait with me until he arrives, if you would like to satisfy your curiosity.'

'I shall certainly help you take your bags down the stairs and please, do call me John.' Once again I had embarrassed myself, but she did not seem to mind a bit.

Thankfully, Tommy was as punctual as he was young and unkempt and I fully understood the source of Miss Sinclair's amusement. If Tommy was to prove to be my only competition, I was certainly standing upon solid ground. Before long her baggage was aboard the trap and I helped her up into her seat, albeit with reluctance. Our final exchange was lingering and silent.

I stood there alone, long after the trap had turned the corner and disappeared from sight.

The thought of Sophie Sinclair making

an early return from Frinton refuelled my determination to bring the matter of the unholy trinity to a swift conclusion. With that in mind, I decided to abandon the lumbering train back to Baker Street in favour of a cab with the command to make all speed!

Holmes had not seemed to be so motivated when I had last seen him, so I was most anxious to discover what news, if any, he had of his brother's whereabouts and the nature of any plans that he had since set in motion. I charged up the stairs upon my return and was aghast to discover that Holmes was nowhere to be seen!

I was about to question Mrs Hudson, when she arrived unannounced at the door.

'Oh Dr Watson, Mr Holmes has gone!' she announced nervously.

'Gone? Gone where, Mrs Hudson?' Mrs Hudson was clearly taken aback by the suddenness of my response, so I invited her to take a chair by the fire.

'Oh Dr Watson, I am so worried about Mr Holmes. You know him better than any man alive and yet even you do not understand his behaviour at times. I cannot tell you where he has gone, because I am the last person in whom he would confide.'

To calm her agitation, I poured her out a small glass of sherry and I waited a moment or two to allow the drink to take its effect before I questioned her further. 'If you explain to me exactly what happened, I might be able to establish his whereabouts. We have been working on several different cases of late. However, I do not understand why this has upset you so; after all of these years you must be used to his erratic behaviour by now?' I reasoned.

Mrs Hudson took a moment or two to gather her thoughts and she drained her glass before continuing.

'Shortly after you left, I noticed Mr Holmes become more and more restless as he awaited the replies to his messages. He was constantly calling down to me to enquire and I realized that he was under a good deal of strain. When he was not shouting to me, I could hear him endlessly pacing up and down, here in front of the fire.

'The wires simply would not arrive, until finally, when I was at the point of despair, he received a message from that cabby fellow, Mr King. Mr Holmes read through it with great excitement and an instant later he was tearing down the stairs! It was a good hour before he finally made his return. Oh Dr Watson, when he did, I was shocked by his appearance, I can tell you.

'I have absolutely no idea as to what kind of an adventure King had led Mr Holmes upon, but I am certain that it involved some kind of danger. He had lost his hat, his coat was splattered with mud, his tie was half undone and there was a small gash of blood upon his left cheek! I have never seen him so angry, Dr Watson. He hurled his coat down onto the floor and he was most discourteous to me when he refused my attention to his cut.' Mrs Hudson was quite flushed with excitement by the time that she had finished her account.

'It certainly sounds like an assignment

that I should have been a part of and I blame myself for having deserted him at such a time. I suppose he gave you no clue as to the nature of his encounter?' I asked, but I could see from her face that my question was a redundant one.

'I am afraid not, Dr Watson, he just took to his chair once more and refused to partake of anything that I offered to him, until the replies arrived to his stupid wires. When they did finally come, it was both of them at once. Mr Holmes asked me to remain, in case he needed to make an immediate reply.

'Surprisingly though, instead of replying to them, he tore them up into a thousand pieces and threw them both onto the fire! It was most peculiar, because he continued to stare at the fire until he was quite certain that both wires had been turned to ash.' I smiled, because Holmes was evidently determined not to make the same mistake twice.

'What did he do after that, Mrs Hudson?'

'Well, to my surprise, he asked me to summon him a cab at once, although he emphasized that under no circumstances was the driver to be Gunner King!'

At first I had been confused by Mrs Hudson's most singular revelation, but I soon realized that, for reasons known only to him, Sherlock Holmes had been determined to cover his traces at any cost. He had previously assured me that I would be at his side right through to the bitter end of this entire affair. I could only assume, therefore, that something had occurred during my absence that had altered his intentions. For the life of me, I could not imagine what that might have been, but I was determined to find out.

'Did Mr Holmes give you any indication as to where he intended to go?' I asked of our long-suffering landlady.

'No, Dr Watson, he disappeared into his room and came out a moment or two later clutching a small overnight bag and his warmest muffler. He was down the stairs and into the cab without offering me a single word of explanation. That is the last that I have seen or heard of him. Oh I do hope that he will be all right.'

'I am sure that he will be fine, Mrs

Hudson,' I offered reassuringly, although I hoped that Mrs Hudson was more convinced by my words of encouragement than I had been! She was on her way to prepare for me a light cold supper, when another thought halted her in her tracks.

'There was another thing he did, that I thought most peculiar at the time. Despite the urgency of his departure, Mr Holmes went to great pains to remove every last trace of chalk from his blackboard, before returning it to his room.'

'Yes, that was a strange thing for him to have done, under the circumstances . . . ' My voice tailed off as I considered her words most carefully. 'Thank you Mrs Hudson!' I called out while she closed the door behind her.

By the time that Mrs Hudson had returned to remove my supper things, I realized that I was no closer to collating my thoughts than I had been before my meal. It was now far too late for me to take any course of action, even if I had one in mind. Therefore, I took a port with my pipe over to the fire, determined to employ Holmes' own method to the problem at hand.

One thing that was immediately obvious to me was the reason behind Holmes' sudden and mysterious departure. He had clearly been most disturbed by his brother's inexplicable disappearance. For Mycroft to even slightly deviate from his customary routine was not only out of character, but it was also unprecedented in all of my experience of the man.

Holmes had been equally mystified by Mycroft's absence, so therefore it was obvious to me that something had occurred during my visit to West Hampstead that had indicated Mycroft's location to my friend and he had acted upon this without a moment's hesitation.

Clearly there was much danger attached to his enterprise, for he had gone out of his way to ensure that I could not follow him. The obliteration of his blackboard, the burning of the wires and his insistence on a cabby other than Gunner King all were indicative of his determination to exclude me from his mission.

Of course there were clues and Bavaria seemed to be the final destination that immediately sprang to mind. Holmes seemed to attach great importance to that principality, for he was galvanized into action from the minute that he received communications from that very place. Had not Menachem Goldman identified a castle there as being the final resting place for the Venetian mandolin?

These facts alone were most indicative, but were they conclusive? I could understand Holmes' desire to journey to Bavaria, but what could possibly have induced such a course of action in his normally immovable brother? Why had he not asked for Holmes to accompany him there? Perhaps to shield him from some unknown danger or was it because Mycroft's involvement with the Diogenes Club and the Bavarian Brotherhood was more clandestine and sinister than even Holmes had thought it to be?

Then again, he had laughed out aloud when I had put that very proposition to him and in retrospect the notion did seem to be a ridiculous one. My head seemed to be reverberating, so I drained my glass and replaced my pipe with a cigarette.

This case had been unique in all of my experiences with Holmes. Never before had we tackled anything of this scale and Holmes had assured me of my involvement throughout and that he would never again tackle an adversary of the dastardly magnitude of a Moriarty for example without me being by his side. I convinced myself, therefore, that before too long and by whatever means that he was able to employ, Holmes would get word to me this time.

With this consolation for comfort I decided to retire for the night, determined to search through every agony column that I could find in the following morning's newspapers.

When my search revealed nothing on the first morning, I merely shrugged off the disappointment, having reached the conclusion that, in all probability, Holmes was still engaged in his travels. Notwithstanding this, I was determined to put my own plans into action and asked Mrs Hudson to despatch Billy the butcher's boy in a search for Gunner King. I reasoned that if any man alive could locate Holmes' mysterious cabby, it would be he.

I next searched through my notes for the address of Denbigh Grey. Evidently, Holmes had attached great value to the messages that Grey had discovered, so much so in fact that the removal of the blackboard had been Holmes' very last action, prior to his departure. Consequently I was certain that a clue must have been evident upon the board.

Grey's landlady had directed me to his local library and there I found him, entombed behind a monolithic pile of ancient books and manuscripts. He greeted me with a mixture of surprise and dismay and before he would even consider talking to me, I had to assure him that neither Daxer nor Irving had suddenly come back from the dead!

With much relief, Grey led me through the back door of the library and we entered the sanctuary of a small private garden that sat behind the building. We shared a wooden bench as I explained the reasons for my visit.

'I should tell you that Mr Holmes is not a man who is prone to revealing his thoughts and theories to others, until he is absolutely certain of his facts. Now that he has disappeared, not for the first time I should add, it has fallen to me to pick up the pieces of his investigation and trace him before he comes to any harm. Is there any clue that you can furnish me with that might aid me in unravelling the code hidden in the manuscript?' I asked of the diminutive scholar.

Denbigh Grey eyed me sympathetically, but he seemed to be as much at a loss as I was. He slowly shook his head before replying.

'You see, Dr Watson, the only thing that the various anomalies had in common was their incongruity. Historically there is no connection between Rameses and Nearchus, for example. Therefore I am certain that the clue cannot possibly be a chronological one.'

'I understand, but I should point out that after several attempts at breaking the code, Mr Holmes abandoned all of his efforts from the moment that you presented us with the clue of Nearchus. He swept all traces from his board and intimated that he no longer had need of it. Was there anything unique within the Nearchus clue that might have caused him to abandon his work at that point?' I asked desperately, although I was met with a similarly negative response.

'My own scholastic curiosity has led me to delve even deeper into the manuscript and I can tell you that the fifth anomaly is no more revealing than the others. This was a reference to the debauched Roman Emperor Elagabalus, who had ruled the empire for a very brief period, some five hundred years after the death of Alexander!'

I must admit that I had never previously heard of this individual, but I was sure that Grey had been certain of his facts. Then Grey pulled a small notebook out of his briefcase and wrote down the name of each clue in broad capital letters.

GARGOYLES
RAMESES

ULYSSES
NEARCHUS
ELAGABALUS

We read down this list of names together and also across with equal care, however we concluded this brief study with neither of us being any the wiser.

'I am sorry that I cannot be of any further use to you, Dr Watson,' Grey said as he slowly rose from the bench.

'May I keep this?' I asked while pointing at the sheet of notepaper.

'Of course and may it serve you well,' Grey smiled.

I thanked him for his time, but I could not help feeling somewhat deflated as I made my way back to Baker Street.

That night my sleep proved to be a most fitful affair. The five names continually reverberated around the inside of my head, each time presenting themselves to me in a variety of different permutations. None of these made any sense to me and as the night slowly turned into a chill and murky dawn, I realized that any further thoughts of sleep would inevitably prove to be futile.

I made my way to the news vendor while the streets were still relatively empty and I had dismissed all of the papers as useless, long before Mrs Hudson had appeared with my breakfast. For once I could understand that feeling of frustration and impatience that my friend had so often experienced and displayed. Mrs Hudson was both disappointed and surprised as she removed my plate of food and discovered that it had been barely touched!

'Oh Dr Watson, you simply cannot afford to let this matter effect you so. You will be of no use to anyone if you do not take some food.'

I smiled at her warning, for I had heard it so often in the past when she had directed it at Holmes.

'I apologize, Mrs Hudson, but I assure you that it does not reflect on your cooking. I suppose that there has been no word yet from Gunner King?' I asked speculatively.

She shook her head sadly.

'No not yet, but I will be up here with

347

it, the instant that it arrives,' she assured me.

So the long wait continued. I occupied my time by bringing Holmes' blackboard out from his room once more and setting out the five names in a variety of different permutations. After several frustrating hours, when I was at the point of abandoning my project and putting Holmes' board away again, I saw it!

It had been so obvious that at first glance I dismissed my conclusion as nothing more than the merest fancy. Then I applied one of Holmes' favourite proverbs to my problem. 'Once you have eliminated the impossible, anything that remains, no matter how improbable, has to be the truth.'

I suddenly realized that I had no further need for that reply from King. I was almost certain now that I knew exactly where I had to journey to. It suddenly all made the most perfect sense.

The idea of someone designing the various crimes with which we had recently been confronted merely to lure Holmes into his web, the castle in

Bavaria, to which the Venetian mandolin had been despatched, the mysterious owner of the castle, shrouded in a black silk mask. Holmes had been correct from the very beginning. Denbigh Grey's anomalies had indeed been the key throughout.

Now all I had to do was await a message from Holmes to let me know that he and his brother were both safe and well before embarking upon this new adventure. Assuming, of course, that it was indeed the case. I was certain that on this occasion, Holmes had no intention of leaving me hanging on a limb, as he had after the Reichenbach confrontation.[1] I consoled myself with the thought that three days was certainly not three years!

However, when the following morning came and there was still no identifiable clue in the agony columns, my impatience soon changed into a state of dire concern. Why would he not write? All manner of explanations occurred to me, each one of them more alarming than the last and I found myself having to confirm my findings upon the blackboard once again.

There was no doubting my conclusions. The first letters of each name spelt out just one thing: GRUNER!! The name itself conjured up such dark and disturbing memories for me that my fear for the safety of the Holmes brothers increased tenfold at the mere thought of the man.

Baron Gruner, otherwise known as 'The Austrian Murderer',[2] had been one of Holmes' most devious and repugnant adversaries. He had been as avid a collector of porcelain as he had been of women. The obvious difference between his twin obsessions was the fact that he did not discard or destroy the porcelain.

Oil of vitriol had been his vicious tool of choice, but it had also proved to be his undoing, for one of his victims had actually turned his weapon upon him and with horrific results. Now he hid his abhorrent scars behind a silken black mask and warded off the outside world with an unassailable castle. Was he the third member of the trinity? I did not know with any certainty, but he was obviously hell-bent on taking out his torment and exacting his revenge upon

Sherlock Holmes.

My resolve was to reach the castle of Neuschwanstein in Bavaria before Gruner had a chance to do so. I was now also certain that it had been none other than Mycroft who had arranged for the early release of Roger Ashley, merely so that he would lead him directly into the lair of his malevolent employer. If that had been the case, then it was almost inevitable that Mycroft had already fallen into Gruner's clutches and that Holmes was almost certainly walking into a trap.

I packed my bag and serviced my revolver without a second's further delay. Even if there was to be no message for me hidden within the columns of the following morning's papers, I was determined to instigate my departure on the first available train. I brought out my Bradshaw and then went downstairs to explain my intentions to Mrs Hudson.

I informed Inspectors Bradstreet and Lestrade by way of a wire of the exact circumstances of Holmes' disappearance and of my immediate intentions. I also included a request that they should prevent Sophie Sinclair from returning to West Hampstead until they had been informed of our safe return.

Then, satisfied that all of my arrangements were in place, I retired for the night.

I continued with my now familiar routine of scouring the agony columns in the morning and I was on the point of abandoning the Telegraph to the same fate as the other disappointing newspapers, when I saw it!

It was only a tiny entry, but I was certain of its origin. It was addressed to the friends of Taharka. Only Holmes and I knew of the significance of that name, for Taharka had been the felucca pilot with whom I had formed a strong and unique bond during our adventures in Egypt. The message read as follows:

DO NOT FEAR, FOR MY BROTHER
AND I ARE BOTH WITHIN THE
VERY SAFEST OF HANDS.
SIGURDSON

The meaning of this was immediately

clear to me. Evidently Holmes had located his brother before any harm had come to him and they both felt secure in each other's company.

That the message was from Holmes was indicated by the name of the correspondent. Sigurdson had been the name of the Norwegian explorer whose personality Holmes had assumed during his three-year absence back in 1891.

I wasted no time in informing Mrs Hudson that her favourite tenant was alive and well and then set out for the station to begin my search for Sherlock and Mycroft Holmes . . .

Notes

Prologue:

[1] *Sherlock Holmes and the Unholyist Trinity* by PDG.

[2] From *The Adventure of Black Peter* by ACD.

[3] From *The Lost Files of Sherlock Holmes* by PDG.

[4] A small sailing vessel of ancient design, often used on the Nile.

[5] Founded by Saint Mark in AD 41.

[6] A part of the Gnostic Codex.

[7] *The Unholy Trinity* by PDG.

Chapter 1:

[1] Mentioned in *The Adventure of the Solitary Cyclist* by ACD.

Chapter 2:

[1] From *The Annals of Sherlock Holmes* by PDG.

Chapter 3:

[1] *The Bruce Partington Plans* by ACD.

We do hope that you have enjoyed reading this large print book.

Did you know that all of our titles are available for purchase?

We publish a wide range of high quality large print books including:
**Romances, Mysteries, Classics
General Fiction
Non Fiction and Westerns**

Special interest titles available in large print are:
**The Little Oxford Dictionary
Music Book, Song Book
Hymn Book, Service Book**

Also available from us courtesy of Oxford University Press:
**Young Readers' Dictionary
(large print edition)
Young Readers' Thesaurus
(large print edition)**

For further information or a free brochure, please contact us at:
**Ulverscroft Large Print Books Ltd.,
The Green, Bradgate Road, Anstey,
Leicester, LE7 7FU, England.
Tel:** (00 44) **0116 236 4325
Fax:** (00 44) **0116 234 0205**

[2] A form of slang that was a mixture of Hebrew and German.

Chapter 8:
[1] The Church of Mary Magdalene, also known as the Hanging Church.

Chapter 9:
[1] Mysteriously, the use of the Shoreditch Mortuary was never satisfactorily explained.

Chapter 11:
[1] From *The Final Problem* by ACD.

Chapter 12:
[1] From *The Illustrious Client* by ACD.